THE WEBBING CLOAK

THE THIRD CRYSTAL KINGDOM NOVEL

RAYMOND S FLEX

1

ANATOMY OF AN ARMY

THE AIR that flowed through the mountain passes was warm now, and it came in little gusts, as if sourced at some volcano, or wafted off a smoking geyser. Whereas the clouds above before had been grey, matted, and clumped-up, now they were black-bottomed, almost as black as the Sable Mountains gathered all around.

Ma'reygar gripped his staff all the tighter and knew that the very natural world was seeing and reacting to his power. Change was in the air, of that he was certain, and he would be its agent, he would drive it forwards and for once bring justice across the land. Bring a new kindness to the Kingdom of Shellacnass, and it would be as beautiful as it would be brutal. He would see to that.

His charges, hundreds of them, all swarmed their way up the coal-shaded rock faces, like angry red ants spilled out from a mound of dirt. He felt his skin tingle because though he had often thought of this day—often *imagined* it—he had never allowed himself to leave it to bear fruit in his mind. He had always kept it at an arm's length. But now, unless his eyes and memory deceived him, it was all coming true.

The dream he had never dared dream.

Because now *he* had regained his rightful place in the Magical Council, now *he* was High Chair of the Magical Council once more .. . and, once again, fire was the dominant force on the Council, he had seen to that, had made it a condition of his acceptance to lead an army up against King Herimyre's mortal one. As a condition of his leading a charge on Ilsnare: the *Crystal* City . . . what a frivolous name. Perhaps once he sat upon the throne *he* would see to its changing.

That warmth plunged through him and he tasted the deep ash as it settled on his tongue, as the ash drifted down from the heavens as sooty snow. And, like a child, he poked his tongue out from between his lips and caught it there. Only when he realised his shoulders shuddering slightly did he notice that he was laughing, deep and unshakable guffaws which ploughed through his chest.

That sulphuric scent on the air too. He had often overheard other mages—*ice* mages—describe it as the stench of rotten eggs. But, for Ma'reygar, nothing could be further from the truth. He only smelled fierce victories there: hard fought and well won.

As he breathed in deeply, his lips still curled back in a smile, he heard that warming howl of the wind as it brushed past him once again. And he watched it brush against the cloaks of his charges, all of them clambering their way up the face of the mountain on which he stood, all of them growing closer with each step. Already he could read the pain and near exhaustion sketched on their faces.

But, if they were to be successful in battle, they needed to know just what it would take. That they'd need more than just their magical proficiency if they wished to defeat Herimyre's army, if they wished to restore *true* balance to the world.

He watched the first few of the mages clambering their way up the final incline, their hands were cut up from climbing, their fingers coated with blood, fresh and dried alike, and their hair all mussed up.

He sucked in that sweet sulphur air and took it down deep into his lungs till it stung the base of his chest, and thickened his blood. He imagined his blood like molten lava, stirring and thickening inside his veins. Only making him stronger.

He turned his attention to the first of the mages coming up over the final rocky ground. Something about the mage's appearance struck him as odd right away. From the hand, that slender, pale, *fragile* hand, the one this mage seemed to favour, he could see that the climb up the mountain had had no effect, that he was just as intact as *clean* as he might've been expected to be from weeks spent down in the Magical Council, in those steaming-hot, soapy, herb-infused baths.

That wasn't what he had wanted from this exercise at all. He had wanted the mages to bleed, every last one of them. He had wanted them to know pain.

Pure *physical* pain.

And that was why he had explicitly forbidden them—*any* of them—to use their magic. Because he knew that when they arrived to Ilsnare, and they came under the influence of Herimyre, and under the influence of his sword—*Tysron*—that they couldn't count upon their magic. They'd need to count upon their *physical* hardiness.

Just as Ma'reygar had made clear when he had briefed his charges, any attempt at cheating his exercise would be met with a succinct yet *brutal* execution. Because that was what wartime required. There could be no subordinance.

To them *he* was the king of their bodies, both physical and magical.

He clutched his staff all the tighter, and kept his gaze level, still fixed right onto that first mage, several steps ahead of the others, and already steadying himself up onto his feet. Attempting to straighten his back, and to walk proudly despite his obvious fatigue.

But Ma'reygar knew that it might well be an act, that *this* mage had all but certainly used magic to aid him up the mountain. That he had *disobeyed* him.

He caught another glance of that fragile, smooth hand, and those simple, sleek fingers, and he clasped all the tighter to those rutted finger marks of his staff, and felt his eyelids droop down almost of their own volition. And he felt the stirring of the clouds over his head, and the heat warming his cheeks, the fire bubbling through his veins.

Since this mage was the first one to disobey him he would make it a true spectacle.

A spectacle that *none* of the others would ever forget.

He would be sure of that.

Just as his eyelids flickered, and he prepared himself to unleash the full force of his hex, he caught sight of the face, the face within the hood of the cloak. And he saw who it was.

Hildie?

Ma'reygar felt the magic pumping through him, sending his heart into a frenzy. He had already reached the point where he was unsure whether or not he would be able to stop. The magic was almost too powerful for him, almost tore him from both directions so as to make the rest of the world almost unseeable to him.

Because now he saw into the magical realm.

All iridescent tones and swirling vortexes.

And yet something, something buried deep inside of him, forced him to grip all the harder on his staff, and to point its blistered tip up towards the heavens, in the direction from which the magic had come down to him.

It fizzled long and hard through the air.

When it hit the clouds above it emitted an almighty thunderclap.

And then echoed long and hard throughout the mountains all around.

That sulphur scent clasped tight over his mouth and nostrils, almost choking itself down his throat, becoming an invisible clod sinking his tongue to the base of his mouth. His tongue felt a throbbing sting pass through it, and he felt the wind knocked out of his lungs.

And then the sheer power of his effort knocked him off his feet, and he fell down onto the hard rocks below.

The rocks pounded his back, and lightning danced up his spine, knotted his muscles, and he felt his heart clench then unclench, as if it was punishing him. Cutting off his blood supply, his *fire* magic, just to show him for whipping up that magical frenzy only to cast it off into the evermore with the mere flick of his wrist.

But he had seen Hildie.

He was sure of it.

That . . . that *mage*, the one who had cheated at his task, who had been the first to clamber up to the top of this mountain, to *use* magic. It had been Hildie.

For the longest time, Ma'reygar lay on his back, feeling every nerve and bone in his body tingle right up to the surface of his skin. And when that feeling was through, a creeping numbness made inroads on his body.

"Father?"

Only when he heard her voice did he begin to feel that sensation subsiding, start to feel the world slowly tilting back to him, coming back to him in waves of detail.

The rock.

Beneath him.

Jutting into his spine.

He reached out with his hands, his withered, old man's hands, leathered from all his travels, and all his experience, sometimes little more sensitive than tree bark. But they served him well enough now, at least enough to let him know that his surroundings were solid, and that he was still joined to this world by the same mortal coil.

When he looked up he saw the clouds all swirling about in his vision, and then his focus drifted, down onto Hildie, as she crouched over him, her lips pressed tightly together, and he eyes already filling with tears. And then he felt those fragile fingers of hers, the ones that had given her magic away, grip his, entwine themselves in his, and he felt his heart warming up once more, and the fire magic within him regaining its control.

Wrestling back against the out-of-control magic which still simmered on the periphery of his consciousness. Nipped at his toes like a winter tide.

"Where . . . where?" Ma'reygar managed to get out.

Hildie tightened her grip on his hand, and he felt her skin

against his reassure him, send those same warm waves through his blood, revitalising him over and over again. And soon he knew that he had the strength to stand.

When he did, he saw that another dozen or so mages had managed to work their way up the mountain, to successfully climb up to Ma'reygar. And he saw, from those emaciated faces, those gnarled-up fingers, the fresh blood which dampened their skin, that they had completed the task to his satisfaction.

He made a note of those faces: grim, weather-hardened, *determined*, and he made a point to count them among his sturdiest followers. These were the ones that he could see his way to trusting when it came to the showdown with Herimyre.

And the hope for the forthcoming battle, for the forthcoming *glorious* victory, was almost enough to knock him off his feet again, and he would've tumbled down if it hadn't been for Hildie's sure hold on him, keeping him upright.

"Come, Father," she said.

And who was he to refuse her?

2

UNSPOKEN TRUTHS

T HE CRACKLING of pig's flesh onto open flames was enough to bring Ma'reygar back to his senses, and to flush out the last of the ringing that passed through his ears after having been knocked back by the flurry of his hex.

Now was his time to stand proud here, before the Magical Council, all of them ready for the feast, their flagons brimming with brandy wine and their cups near to overflowing with ale, and their faces all prickled to attention, their eyes sharp as the tip of Herimyre's sword.

He crunched up the remainder of his toasted bread roll, savouring that buttery goodness there, all its richness that lolled about the inside of his mouth, and his stomach stirring from the irresistible scent of that roasting, suckling pig over on the fire.

As High Chair of the Magical Council it would be his pleasure to have the first slice of the pork, to savour all those sumptuous spiced flavours that some hard-working mage had worked on in the kitchen for hours during the day, while his companions had gone about their task, the task that Ma'reygar had set them.

Ma'reygar had been informed of those mages who hadn't returned from the task. There were only five or six of them, all told, from among the hundreds he had set to the task. Of course, he had excused the members of the Magical Council from taking part, though the idea of them taking part with their withered, bony bodies had somewhat entertained him for a few moments.

But, no, as much as he hated to admit it, he would need them, all of them, for the forthcoming war. He needed as much brute magical strength as he could rightly . . . or *wrongly* . . . get his hands on.

Neither had he put Yunt'ga'boar to the task, though he had been relieved of his position on the Magical Council soon after Ma'reygar had been unanimously voted to become the new High Chair.

Ma'reygar had some pity for the beaten mage, and he knew that, in the field of ice magic, Yunt'ga'boar had almost no equal.

. . . And what was it they said about enemies, and keeping them close? . . .

He glanced to Hildie, sitting at his side, her eyes fixed on her own untouched flagon of brandy wine.

She had been quiet since she had returned to him, since she had greeted him up there on that mountaintop. And he was weary of asking her secrets too soon, of opening up wounds which might still be sore for her. Because he could sense a great sadness lurking over her.

And he had noticed that wound of hers, the way that her left hand had been mutilated, left almost without form or substance. Now he knew why she'd favoured the right when she'd clambered up the mountain, and why she had chosen to use magic.

9

It was quite simple. She hadn't been part of the task at all. She had simply asked another mage where Ma'reygar might be found and then been pointed in his direction. She had had no idea at all.

His poor daughter. And to think that he had almost blown her off the face of the world, and into another. He never—*ever*—would've forgiven himself.

She was all he had left now.

The only person he loved in the whole world.

The only one who could get close to him.

Ma'reygar decided that now was the time, since he was growing hungry. He took a hearty mouthful of brandy wine, swallowed it down, feeling it tickle him all the way, and then he rose up from his seat and glowered out over the Magical Council.

They were all here, all present.

Ems'plot: Ice.

Kwar: Fire.

Lumbswich: Ice.

Grendlin: Fire.

J'plaut: Ice.

Wyd'rswen: Fire.

And just as Yunt'ga'boar had cast Ma'reygar out from the Magical Council, made it so that he would never be privy to the discussions of the Council, Ma'reygar had cast Yunt'ga'boar out also.

Left him to sulk away in his quarters away from the talk.

"Well," Ma'reygar began, "I believe that the task has been somewhat successful in weeding out the weaker of the mages, as well as showing off the stronger ones among us."

The Council remained in total silence. He could see that they were all stricken with terror as they gazed up at him. And that they were too afraid to look away. To busy their attention with the flagons or cups sitting before them.

"And it is also my belief that we are gaining strength, strength enough that we might begin to form up and lead the charge on Ilsnare." He paused a moment for effect, and then added, "By morning."

Even through the residual ringing in his ears, Ma'reygar caught the faint gasps from some of the members of the Council, and he registered those in his mind for later reference. So he would know, ahead of time, who the cowards among them were.

Perhaps he should have swallowed his better judgement after all, and forced them all to take up the task he had assigned the rest of the mages.

At least then he would've known who was the most determined among them to please him. And who were the weaklings.

Ma'reygar continued, "As previously arranged you're all to bring your assigned mages together and to have them organised into their respective troops for the march on Ilsnare, so that they're all ready for the ensuing battle."

With that Ma'reygar reached for his flagon of brandy wine and polished the lot of it off in a single gulp. When he looked back over the table, to the faces of the members of the Council, he caught several of them exchanging glances.

Mutiny?

... Or cold feet?

It always paid to nip either in the bud as quickly as possible.

Something for him to keep an eye on, in any case, though he could hardly see how they would undercut him now. After all, these mages had all voted him back onto the Council in the first place, *they* were the ones who had voted to appoint him to his long-awaited role of High Chair. But he was resilient that it would be *him* who would decide when . . . whether or not . . . he chose to step aside.

And none of them had better stand in his way.

If they knew what was good for them.

With that thought sketched deeply on his mind, Ma'reygar watched as a mage refilled his glass with yet more brandy wine, and then Ma'reygar raised it up. "A toast," Ma'reygar said, making a point of catching each member of the Council in his lingering gaze, watching that slight flinch of the eye, the ill-concealed gulps of cowardice. "To *victory!*"

They all raised their glasses and drank to that.

And Ma'reygar slumped back into his chair, and eyed the rim of his own flagon, the brandy wine dribbling down over the edge of it, and he thought again of that throne, and just how sweet he would feel sat upon it.

After the banquet wound down, and that roast pork sat nicely in Ma'reygar's belly, he watched as each of the members of the Magical Council excused themselves, one by one. He watched each of them go, studying their expressions, attempting to catch their eye as they slunk past him. And he succeeded in most cases.

At least all the fire mages looked him in the eye.

And most of the ice mages.

But he was sure that even those ice mages that had chosen to wander their way off to bed without so much as meeting his eye would bend to his whim sooner or later.

He counted on it.

Soon enough, the only other person sitting with him in the meeting hall was Hildie, his dear daughter. The fireplace that occupied much of one of the walls of the hall now crackled low, its embers glowing a deep orange colour, and the warmth still wafting out in waves, causing Ma'reygar's veins to tingle with magic.

He jabbed his tongue into the backs of his teeth, working loose several morsels of pork that had got themselves stuck there, and he enjoyed swallowing those pieces down almost as much as he'd enjoyed the main course.

All salty, and meaty and sustaining.

He could feel that pork working itself into his muscles, giving them strength, and further warding away the adverse effects of his aborted hex earlier in the day.

When he'd almost cast a hex on his own daughter.

He could feel the weight of a thousand questions on his mind, and he was sure that Hildie had just as many questions for him too. And now was the time, with them alone here, without the curious ears of the Council, for them to speak.

One thing laid heavy on his mind first of all, one thing that he had to know before anything else, and so that was what he started with. "The Webbing Blade," he said. "You have it with you?"

Hildie tilted her face away from his right away, her flame-red hair shimmering in the firelight. And he had his answer.

A flurry of rage burst through Ma'reygar's chest and he barely kept a hold on his anger. It had just sprung up inside of him. But he tried to quieten it down, to reassure himself, to tell himself that he had to think logically, not let his reflexes get the better of him again.

After all, they'd almost been responsible for wiping out his daughter on that mountaintop. He couldn't afford to allow himself to get carried away a second time.

"Where?" he said. "*Where* is it?"

Hildie remained silent, still staring off into mid-air, staring off at the stone wall on the other side of the table.

Ma'reygar's rage won out again, and he lurched forwards, his hand catching Hildie at her chin and dragging her eyes round to look into his. Those emerald-green eyes of hers took on a sheen in the firelight. "I won't ask again," he said.

He felt a tremor pass over Hildie's skin, and her take a snatched breath. She was frightened. He could tell that. But what he wasn't sure of was whether or not she was frightened of *him*.

He looked deeper into those eyes of hers, tried to divine just what was going on in her mind, if she might give something away to him.

He decided to change the direction of his enquiries, and switched his attention to her hand, which she had kept expertly hidden beneath the sturdy wooden table for the duration of the meeting with the Magical Council. And which she still kept hidden now.

"What happened to your hand?" he said.

Hildie remained still for a long moment, and then she struggled and succeeded in casting off his hold on her chin. She rose out of her chair and took a few steps away from him. But she stopped short of leaving the room.

Yes, Ma'reygar knew that she still felt the weight of her respect for him. She still had that. She couldn't simply walk out of the room her father sat in without proper respect and manners.

"*Who* did it to you?" Ma'reygar said.

Hildie stayed almost impossibly still, her red hair still giving off that fire-like sheen, and her lips, despite what must've been a long journey here, to the Seat of the Magical Council, still remained plump and juicy.

He had always imagined that she must drive the boys quite wild.

When she spoke, her voice was so quiet as to make the words almost unintelligible. But Ma'reygar understood. However that name was spoken, he would *always*, till the day he died, understand *that* name. It might've been said in a garbled, feverish dream, but he would always understand it no matter what.

His adversary's name.

The one who had taken his wife away from him.

And the one who he had sworn to kill.

Who he had raised an army to kill.

Herimyre.

3

AN UNWORLDLY STORM

T HE SHIP rose up the crest of yet another wave, rolling its way up, teetering on the top for that primal, precise moment, before it dived down the other side with the waves crashing against the hull as it hit the bottom.

Down here, in the bowels of the boat, Louson Dorf could feel every last lurch of the ship, every last smash of a wave against its seemingly flimsy structure. All around him, the lanterns bobbed back and forth, casting, and recasting, the candlelight over him, and about him. Each time the light came into contact with his skin he felt its sting.

The *sting* of light which had become his very worst nightmare.

Sunlight, fire, candlelight, it made no difference.

It was like the living world was out to get him.

Lou felt the shiver pass over him yet again. That weighty, freezing chill that seemed to haunt him more and more these days. He clutched the sides of his hammock tight in his fists, feeling the knotted-up and sea-gnarled rope against the raw skin of his palms.

His mouth tasted of vomit from the constant puking he'd done in the past day or so, and his stomach felt like it had emptied itself for the final time.

He breathed in that musty woody stench which lingered over the whole ship, but even more so down here, below deck.

A couple of drops of seawater fell onto his face, leaking out through the wooden planks. He tasted their saltiness and the cool chill. The temperature was revitalising in a way, though the salt was totally unwelcome, and only seemed to dry out his throat all the more.

Make his nausea worse.

With another gut-wrenching *creak* of wood, the ship bucked its way down yet another wave, and the flush of the waves poured out over the deck above. Another smattering of drops from the sea splattered down onto Lou's cheeks, and he turned over in his hammock, onto his front, and stared down at his bundled-up belongings that sat nestled below him.

The Webbing Blade.

The Webbing Bow.

And now he was on the trail to finding the Webbing Cloak.

But even with those two magical artefacts close by, *almost* close enough for him to reach out and touch, he still felt the never-ending nausea wreaking havoc with his system, as if he was just a sodden cloth to be wrung out in an uncaring and ferocious fist.

He could feel the pounding at his temples again, and the rising of whatever was left in his stomach . . . because it couldn't be bile . . . and he prepared himself for another retch.

When nothing came out he did his best to sit upright in the hammock, though it was a mostly thankless task, not only due to the material of it, but due to the constant motion of the boat as it jarred over the waves, rocking about constantly.

And to think that, once upon a time, the idea of merely seeing the sea had been a dream to him, and one which he'd desperately wanted to fulfil before he died.

Thinking on it now, though, he might've been happy never to have seen the sea again in his life, if he could just get himself off the ship and back onto dry land.

He heard another of those gut-wrenching *creaks*, and then turned on his side to look to the door of his cabin, and to the figure rounding the door.

His sis.

Syre.

This time he had insisted she come along with him. Though he'd left the others back at the encampments, in the solid hands of Sully and Rut, he hadn't trusted anyone to look after Syre as well as he could. Because only *he* could know just how much she meant to him.

Anyway, just as he'd ordered it, Sully and Rut would be breaking the encampments in the coming days, taking the people away from the foothills of the Sable Mountains, and away from the prospective path of the magical army, of where Hildie might come from.

His heart wrenched a little in his chest and he found himself flinch just a touch. Still thinking about her sent his nerves jangling, and his blood all the more frosty. More because he wished to speak with her, to clear the air between them.

For whatever unspeakable—*unforgiveable*—things she had done in burning down all those villages, he knew that her protective charm over the encampments had saved his people, and that she might just as easily have joined forces with those other mages, have slaughtered those hapless mortals and gone on her way.

Where she was now, he had no way of knowing. But he couldn't help hoping that she was safe, and that she would find somewhere she belonged.

Somewhere she could go and forget all about this brewing magical war.

Gods knew, that was just what Lou was doing. He wanted to get his hands on the Webbing Cloak so that he might meet back up with Sully and Rut and the rest of his people, and guide them onto a better place.

Once he was a fully formed mage, Lou knew that he would be able to offer them his protection from all the evils of the world.

That was his destiny now.

He managed to summon a faint smile for Syre, as he took in her inky black hair. He could only linger over her eyes for a few moments, though, knowing that he simply couldn't shake that image of her he'd seen. Of those *black* eyes of hers that he'd seen when they had both summoned up that protective charm which had seen off the mages.

And the weeks she'd spent in bed recovering from that dark magic which had ripped through her veins.

Which had saved them.

And which had almost killed her.

"How you feeling?" she said, sounding bright, and her eyes ebbing wide too. For some reason none of this seafaring had the same effect on her as it did on him. She was lucky he supposed.

Lou tried to sit up again, but only succeeded in sliding back down in the hammock, feeling weak as anything. Only then did he realise that she held a wooden bowl of warm broth in her hands, steaming away with that herby, meaty smell which had seemed appetising to Lou at the beginning of the journey, but which now almost turned his guts inside out.

Still, he felt his stomach clamouring for a taste, no doubt wanting something to replace all the food he'd expelled.

Just as she got within a few paces of him, the boat lurched off hard to the side, and she skittered over into the side. But she was nimble on her feet, like a cat, and landed against her back, keeping the broth safe from spilling.

As the boat levelled out on the crest of the wave, she tottered over to him and handed him the bowlful of broth. He took it for her. "Thanks," he said.

She gripped a hold of the rope which held his hammock up and watched on as he took the broth down him.

The broth was pretty much how Lou had been told back at the dock, from some ragged traveller who'd just got off the boat they found themselves on. He'd said that the way the ship's kitchen ran —the way that *all* ship's kitchens ran—was that they started off with some great hunks of meat which they boiled the broth out of.

And, after a few weeks at sea, as Lou and Syre had already passed, the meat got so boiled down that the broth that they got from it was pretty much just this greasy, salty slime.

That was the broth that Lou was taking in right now.

But he felt so famished that he simply poured it down his gullet and was done with it. His stomach seemed to feel glad for it, giving him a satisfied little tremble. Then he handed the finished bowl off to Syre.

"Captain says we should be there by dawn," she said.

"Yeah?" Lou said, unable to believe that this voyage might be coming to an end.

"Arriving around midday."

Lou couldn't help but flinch a little at that notion.

Holding the bowl down at her side, Syre seemed to notice this. "But don't worry, you can use my cloak too if you find the sun too much. It'll be fine."

Lou knew that he should've taken their arrival as a blessing because it'd bring an end to this horrific, seemingly never-ending sea voyage. But, at the same time, he had to admit that being down here, in the dank underbelly of the ship, he'd at least been sheltered from the sun for the whole while.

Sometimes he wondered just how his master Auch'ray managed living up there, on the mountaintop, right under the greatest strength of the sun. Since Auch'ray's powers were well advanced, when compared with Lou's, he guessed the effects of the sun must've been a hundredfold . . . or, at least, Lou thought Auch'ray's powers at least a hundred times greater than his own.

"You want some more broth?" Syre said. "I can go fetch some from the kitchen."

Just then, just the word floating out from her mouth, was enough for Lou to leap out of his hammock and rush over to the bucket over in the corner, and bring the broth back up once again.

4

BACK ON SHORE

L OU PASSED the rest of the night in dreamless sleep. He
guessed that it'd been quite a long time since he'd had to
contend with those nightmares about killing the king. Had it been
because he'd solved it in some way?

Days after Hildie had gone and the mages had been sent
scarpering off across the plains, hopefully back to the Sable
Mountains, Lou had met with another hobblesman—and with
this one he'd been very sure to check it *wasn't* Hildie in disguise—
who had informed him of the news. That Herimyre had assumed
the role of king.

That now he'd taken up the mantle in Ilsnare Palace.

After Lou had heard that news, the dream had gone away. Had
it been because he'd known that the figure lurking in the shadows
of the king's quarters in his nightmare had been Herimyre, just
biding his time, ready to take to the throne?

And that crow sitting out there on the branch outside the
window had been Syre? Or at least a representation of the dark

magic which now dwelled in her blood, and which he would have to keep an eye on until the day that he died?

If only he'd paid more attention, thought more about that book he'd burned back at the encampments, if only he'd snatched it out from her grasp and disposed of it sooner, then maybe his sis might've been saved.

But if he had taken the book from her, if she hadn't known of its secrets, then surely those mages, out on the plains, would've made light work of the pitiful protective charm Lou would've managed to conjure on his own. And they all would've been killed.

As Lou rose up onto the deck, with Syre just before him, holding his hand, keeping him steady despite the now calm seas. From beneath his hooded cloak, Lou could see the port of Brinder Island sweeping into view, with its olive-coloured hillsides, and its glistening water lapping at its shores.

The glistening reflections from the *sun*.

Which Lou could still feel the prickle of despite the pair of cloaks—his own and Syre's—that he wore to cover his skin from the worst of it.

But he turned his mind to other things. To the bountiful fruit trees which that same stranger who'd warned Lou about the ship's broth, had also informed him were immensely satisfying to gorge yourself on, and a rare wonder after weeks of ship food.

Lou felt as if someone had gutted him from the inside out, and he guessed, in a way, he had been. When he got onto the island, and they found some lodging, he was determined to sleep this off for a few days, before they needed to go on looking for the Threaded Pit, and for the location of the Webbing Cloak.

That name, the Threaded Pit, was the only hint which Auch'ray had held in front of Lou's nose, the only piece of information he'd had to go on in his search, but it had proved useful.

It'd been easily extracted from some half-cut sailor in a tavern back at the port of Shildersmoore, where they'd caught this boat here, to Brinder Island.

Lou was conscious of the sailors all buzzing around him, of them laughing, slapping one another on the back. And inside he felt that same level jubilation, and their own jubilation seemed to seep in through his skin. But he had no energy to join them in their celebrations. The sun was just too powerful an enemy, pounding him over and over, seemingly heaping wave upon wave of an offensive against him.

But he remembered Auch'ray's lesson well, knew that he *had* to live with his enemy to understand it, and that the key to all-conquering strength was being able to walk with weakness. And yet, at times like these, with the sun on his back, and an empty stomach, it proved a tough lesson for Lou to absorb.

From up at the crow's nest, a sailor called out something several times over, in some sailor's dialect he had no idea how to understand. Though, from what he could gather beneath his hood, they were closing on dry land, and that the ship was turning sharply to the right as it sailed on its way—the fresh island breeze curling back its sails—into the harbour.

Several other ships dotted the harbour, and Lou noted that, unlike the ship they sailed in, most of them were much smaller. Fishermen's vessels. Certainly not designed for the high seas, not for the same voyage they'd just undertaken from Shildersmoore.

Just from looking out from beneath his hood, from breathing in that fresh, fishy, *salty* air, it made him almost whimper for a simpler life, one where he lived out in nature—in the *sunlight*—and without any worries.

But now he had started down the path to becoming an ice

mage that was the one that he'd have to stick to. If he turned away from it now it might destroy him.

That was another lesson which Auch'ray had taught him.

The way that Lou saw things now, it seemed like danger stalked him from every side, sniffing out a weakness, just lurking in the shadows, readying to pounce.

When they disembarked the ship, he was dimly aware of all the farewells that Syre was delivering to, and being delivered by, the various sailors of the ship. He guessed that during the voyage she'd made some friends among them. On those calmer nights, from below deck, in his hammock, swaying lightly with the motion of the boat, Lou recalled hearing snatches of her singing with the men, and of her singing alone, and them listening to her.

Every time she had finished a song, one of those mournful ballads, the ones that Endmere, his hometown burned to the ground, had been famous for—and which were now lost except for being in hearts and minds, and on the tongues, of a fair few dozen of the survivors—the sailors had burst into a frenzy of applause and clapping and whistling.

Those first few nights Lou had almost convinced himself that she might be in some sort of danger, and that he should go to her rescue. But a little while later it had dawned on him that these sailors were much more akin to young, curious, home-sick boys, and that they were really no threat at all.

He guessed that while the magical blood in his veins might thicken or thin accordingly, that dumb heroic streak within him would be much tougher to extinguish.

If he ever wished it extinguished, that was.

They picked out a place in the port town, and the largest settlement on the island, Irmlesbrook, though Lou was pretty much just a passenger to whole the process. Only once Syre had got the drapes drawn and the sunlight flushed out of the room did Lou begin to feel the sharp, *poisonous*, effect of the sun on his system begin to wane.

And he saw fit to taking off one of the cloaks, to laying it out on the bed where it rustled up against the rough blanket.

He stood there for a long while, absorbing the room, looking to the two twin beds sitting side by side. Though the place seemed clean enough, Lou couldn't help but smell dust in the air, feel dust brushing up against his skin. And he could still feel the empty burn of bile at the back of his throat. The sooner he got something substantial to eat the better.

Then he could start thinking of the Webbing Cloak.

His hunger, though, wasn't sufficient to chase him out of their bedroom before the sun set on Brinder and Lou was quite sure that the darkness outside was complete. Then he woke Syre, and the two of them descended through the guesthouse and headed out into the streets of Irmlesbrook.

The largest tavern in town, or at least the most boisterous, was named the *Peddy Nickle*, and Lou simply followed his nose, allowing it to guide him along the crooked, unpaved street, with the pebbles which seemed to be constantly scattering about, bouncing off his boots. He had the Webbing Blade down at his hip, concealed beneath his cloak. He had opted to leave the hood of his cloak down. He savoured the feel of the moonlight against his bare neck and against his cheeks. It was almost the same as that feeling he used to get out in the fields, when he'd been a working hand, and he'd felt the sun shining down on his shoulder blades.

Energising him.

Back when he'd been a working hand, the moon had meant danger and fear, that at any moment a cursed animal might bound out from a bush and catch his flesh in its jaws.

Now, though, the night-time, to Louson, represented safety and comfort.

A rare refuge.

As they crossed the threshold of the *Peddy Nickle*, Lou could smell the hearty scent of chicken being roasted over a fire. From what he'd heard about Brinder, the island was such a long way off the mainland of Shellacnass, any *real* world, that there were no cattle or pigs on the island. That the people preferred to use their land for crops, and to keep chickens, which weren't such a load on the boats that would have to carry them to the island.

Lou admired their autonomy, and knew, at the same time, that he and his people were just finding their feet now. Because, before, they had relied on Ilsnare, being a village on the surrounding plains of the Crystal City, to bring them whatever luxuries they'd grown accustomed to.

It appeared to Lou that the people of Brinder had learned well to live without luxury. And they seemed happy enough about it.

As Lou had learned over many years of visiting out-of-town taverns and public houses, he kept to the periphery, kept to the shadows. He knew how a stranger could very easily disrupt the sensitive equilibrium of a place such as this, simply from not knowing his role.

Lou recalled once, when he'd been walking home from a field in the early afternoon, having been allowed home early by Old

Man Junth, how he'd somehow got himself lost. He'd been so used to taking a cart from Endmere to the fields that he just hadn't thought much about where he'd been heading.

And when he'd walked into that tavern to ask directions from the landlord, shining his smile at just about everyone, with that stench of stale ale cutting through the gloomy, woody air, and making his stomach quiver, he recalled the cold silence which'd greeted his request.

And then someone had spat at Lou's feet, claimed that Lou had an Ilsnare accent, and that they *hated* people from Ilsnare.

Lou had caught a clue at that point and departed the tavern quickly. But he hadn't forgotten the lesson. Soon after, he found the road to Endmere by asking a local sheep farmer, and had got back on track.

Still lurking in the shadows, consciously keeping his body in front of Syre's, so that if an attack came he would be ready to block it, and also keeping one hand on the handle of the Webbing Blade the whole time, he skulked along taking in the bar area.

Full tonight, the babble of conversation seemed to rise like a thick cloud about the place. Glasses tinkled together in celebration and then were slammed down, empty, onto the bar almost as fast.

Lou could already taste the sour note of the ale on his tongue, almost overpowering that smell of roasting chicken which had brought them in here in the first place.

From the fireplace, over in the corner of the tavern, blazing away, crackling up as it burned through the logs, he could feel waves of heat begin to affect him. Just as the sun affected him.

He counted fourteen patrons at the tavern that night, all with their backs turned towards them. Well, that gave them the advantage, Lou supposed. Next, he caught the barman's eye.

The barman's age, more than anything else, caught Lou off guard. He supposed that he had been expecting someone much older, at least all the barmen he'd met in his life had been older. For what the barman didn't have in age, he seemed to make up for in bushy black hair.

Though his skin was tight, and youthful, and his lips rosy red, he had thick eyebrows, like a pair of well-scrubbed brooms, and a thatch of hair which seemed to jut out all over, finally coming to an end halfway down his spine . . . or so it seemed to Lou.

The barman didn't smile either, though he did wipe his hands clean on his well-stained apron and strut off along the bar to meet with Lou at the other side. He had a gruff-sounding voice that sounded put on, and Lou guessed that this man was trying to make a run of seeming older than he truly was. "Watcha want?"

"Food," Lou said, his voice sounding grainy and at least half as exhausted as he felt.

The barman nodded. "We got food." He snorted phlegm. "You got money?"

Feeling a little frailer, the long sea voyage still catching up with him, Lou nodded. He felt Syre sidling up beside him and taking hold of his arm, sinking her nimble fingers into his cloaked wrist. Then she whispered in her ear, "It's okay, Lou, don't worry. I know all these people. They're sailors—from the ship. You don't have to act all inconspicuous now."

Lou flashed a quick glance along the bar, to the patrons all sitting there. While he half-recognised some of their faces, others were totally unfamiliar to him. But what had he expected considering that he'd spent the majority of the voyage sealed off below deck?

He did trust his sis, though, and so made a point of being a little more forthcoming, a little more confident. He looked hard and square at the barman. "And we're also interested in knowing just how to get to the Threaded Pit."

It was like a hex had gone off in the centre of the tavern, like it had sparked into the air and struck each and every one of the patrons seated at the bar. And they all, as one, went totally silent, and turned on their stools to stare at Lou.

And Lou stared right back at them, his fingers locking tight to the handle of the Webbing Blade, loosening the dagger from its sheath.

5

A STICKY SITUATION

THIS HAD BEEN A MISTAKE. A big mistake. Lou knew that now. The way that all the patrons were looking at him, *staring* at him, let him know that he'd done something totally wrong.

He thought about where they were, in the middle of the sea. Why, there was no law or order here, other than the loose morals which the sailors brought with them.

He glanced to Syre, seeing if she'd noticed it too. But she didn't look shocked in the least. In fact, she was smiling.

He followed her gaze, traced it to those disgruntled faces of the sailors, all sitting at the bar, and he could hardly believe her reaction. He leaned into her and said, "I think we'd better go."

She met his eyes briefly. "No, it's fine. Trust me."

He looked back over the sailors once again, and they all remained staring over at them. Frowns sketching their lips, their cups of ale clasped in their fists. And, Lou was sure, their muscles almost bulging out from the sleeves of their tunics.

Syre spoke up. "That's right," she said. "We're looking for the Threaded Pit. This here is Louson Dorf, Ice Mage, and he's in search of the Webbing Cloak. That's why we've come to Brinder Island."

The silence was just as steely as it had been before, and it was only punctuated by the occasional crackle of logs on the fire, the *spit* of grease escaping from one of the chickens rotating at the end of its rod.

And despite the situation, despite these hardy sailors all staring them down, looking like they'd be ready to fix them in a moment, Lou felt his stomach give a quiet *growl* of hunger. He could almost taste that chicken flesh in his mouth now. The ashy smell of the chicken was almost overwhelming for him. He squeezed the handle of the Webbing Blade a little tighter, as much to help ward off his hunger as to guard against any attack from one of these sailors.

No one moved to speak, and Lou observed the barman's eyes flickering about their sockets, apparently unsure just where to look. He knew that the look the barman wore now was a weary one—one that knew the symptoms of a forthcoming bar fight when it saw one.

And he saw one now.

Lou half-expected him to duck down behind the bar.

"Does *any*one know how to reach the Threaded Pit?" Syre said, her voice even louder now, deeper even.

And that sent a tingle through Lou's nerves, reminded him of when he'd looked up to her back on the plains and seen those jet-black eyes of hers—those *pit*-black eyes of hers—as they'd seen off those mages together.

With the protective charm they'd summoned together.

Still, the sailors kept up their glum expressions. No one moved to answer. No one even moved to bring their cup of ale to their lips. And it was then that Lou saw the barman bow his head towards them.

"Gotta keep quiet about the Threaded Pit," he said.

"And why's that?" Lou said, breaking his silence, and trying to ignore the group stare from every sailor sat at the bar.

The barman wrinkled up his nose, then looked back at the bar. He sniffed hard and then, his voice this time going a little shrill, giving way to maybe what was his natural tone of voice—the one he didn't fake so as to sound older—he said, "All right, they don't mean nothing by it. Back to your drinks you lot."

Lou felt those words hang in the air, almost *ring* through his ears. Another waft of the scent of that cooking chicken lingered in his nostrils, turned his tongue to butter, and he watched as, one by one, the sailors turned their attention back to their ale. And, even more gradually, back to their conversations.

Voice by voice, the familiar babble from before started up again, and Lou allowed his shoulders to fall in relief.

He slid his hand away from the handle of the Webbing Blade and listened tight to just what the barman had to say.

Before the barman continued his explanation, with the bar now back to approaching its noise level from before, he slipped off and unskewered one of those juicy-looking chicken breasts from over at the fireside.

Lou watched him, with his tongue just about bathing itself in saliva, as he sliced it up into a pair of bowls with a shiny, long-bladed knife, and then brought the meat over to the two of them.

"Ale to drink?" the barman said, his eyes shifting between the two of them.

Lou exchanged glances with his sis. "Not for me, thanks."

Syre's mouth quivered, just a little, and he saw a little of that rebelliousness just below the surface of her eyes, that slight streak that he had noticed coming out more and more these days. She was just testing the waters.

She looked back to the barman. "For me neither."

The barman grunted, and then trudged off to a bucket rank with mould on the outside, but the light of the bar too dark to see the contents of the inside, and he took a pair of wooden cups, dunked both into it, and withdrew the liquid.

As he came back over to them, the liquid spilled out over the sides, splashing on the floor. And Lou could already smell the tangy scent of the liquid inside of those cups. He was on the verge of placing it—perhaps having tasted it off some hobblesman who'd drifted once through Endmere—when the barman unravelled the mystery for him.

"Lemon-laced water," he said. "Good for your guts." His lips curled a little in a smile. "Cleans out your insides."

Lou guessed that, after that sea voyage, and all the vomiting he'd done, he really didn't need to 'clean' his insides all that much. But he took a sip anyway, and instantly he felt his mouth alive with the zest of the fruit. Unlike anything else he'd ever tasted. Though he might've tasted some drink like this before, he'd never had it so *fresh*.

"Picked off the trees this morning," the barman said, with another snort, as if answering the question on Lou's mind.

It stung a little too, and Lou felt it sting its way all round his mouth, then all down his throat, then down to his guts, which gave a little quibble when the drink reached there. But he soon turned his attention back to the succulent-looking, smoking chicken breast all sliced up in the bowl before him. With no sign of cutlery, he decided to use his fingers. And it didn't seem like the barman was in any mood to complain.

As the two of them scoffed through their chicken, the barman lowered his voice, at least made it low enough so that no one would overhear. "Like I said," he began. "Gotta take a bit of care speakin' about the Threaded Pit on Brinder Island. There's a lotta legend floatin' about the place, if you get what I mean."

Lou chewed up his mouthful of chicken breast, saw that he only had another slice to go, and then swallowed. "No," he said, "I can't say I do."

The barman's lips twitched into a smile, and a few creases appeared round his eyes, digging into his youthful skin. Lou guessed that all those creases had been engrained there from one too many late nights. Whereas the creases Lou had on his own face were from one too many early mornings. They were like two sides of the same coin in some ways, the barman and him.

"Oh, there's been a loada talk about the Threaded Pit. Why, I grew up here, on Brinder, I ran about the hills here, searchin' and such. Never thoughta goin' into sailing, though most other people I grew up with did. Never could get my sea legs, if ya know what I mean?"

If the barman meant anything about getting nauseous at sea, then Lou knew exactly what he meant.

"Anyway, the Threaded Pit, it's this place"—he brought up his arm and extended a skinny finger out over Lou's shoulder—"rocks and such, out thar, mile or so out from the island, or so it's known."

"And why're people afraid of it?" Lou said, glancing to Syre, seeing that she was just as engrossed in the barman as he was.

"*Sailors* are afraid of it because it's where they wreck their ships." The barman glanced round over his shoulder, and Lou saw that one of the sailors sitting at the bar had turned and was looking at them intently. This didn't seem to break the barman's flow this time, though. "Whenever there's a storm, or the currents, they go a changin', as they've wont to do once in a while, why a ship can find itself gettin' good and cut up on those rocks. Stranded out there, on the brink of the Threaded Pit."

Lou stared off over the barman's shoulder, to that sailor staring at them. The sailor made no move to look away from them, or any move to reach for his cup of ale before him. Lou spoke to the barman while still meeting the sailor's eye. "And why's that such a bad thing? Doesn't anyone come out to rescue shipwrecked sailors from the rocks?"

The barman gave a throaty chuckle. "Ah, no, no, fella. Thing is, whenever any ship goes out there a rescuin' the day after any wreck, go out to them rocks, to the brink of the Threaded Pit, they find nothing at all."

"Or maybe they just didn't make it to the rocks, maybe they drowned at sea?"

The barman shook his head. "Nah, more often than not they find the evidence. The *footprints* in the sand, at the entrance to the cave mouth."

"Maybe they took shelter in the cave."

The barman broke out into full-on laugh, a laugh that almost blasted Lou clean off his barstool, but he somehow clung on. And when he looked down to the last slice of chicken breast, still sitting at the base of his bowl, he found that somehow he'd lost his appetite.

Maybe it'd been something in the drink the barman had given him. He hadn't been accustomed to fresh anything for the past few weeks at sea so it would be no wonder that his body might well reject it.

"More chicken?" the barman said.

Lou slipped a sidelong glance at Syre, saw her give him the merest glimmer of a nervous smile, and then he nodded.

As the barman shifted off to go fetch some more chicken from the fireplace, Lou noticed the sailor that'd been staring at them all along slip off his barstool and strut his way towards them.

Lou reached for the handle of the Webbing Blade and got himself into the mind-set that would allow him to kill.

If he *had* to.

The sailor had a raggedy blond beard, and a rumbling gut. As he approached them he hitched up his ever-falling trousers a good half dozen times. And he belched almost as much.

Everything about this, about this approaching sailor, made Lou wary. He slipped the Webbing Blade clean out from its sheath and felt the tingle of the chill from its blade.

He felt better now.

Prepared.

Ready to protect himself and Syre.

As the sailor got closer still, Lou could see that he wore a smirk in the gloomy barroom light, and that he had a little ale still clinging to his lips, sparkling in the firelight. Before Lou could think about much anything else, the sailor jutted his hand out, a handful of stubby, weathered fingers. "Friend of Auch'ray, brother?" he said.

Lou was stunned for just a few moments. He stared at those calloused hands, just as calloused as his own were from his earlier life of being a working hand, though he guessed this sailor also had a fair amount of salt rubbed into his skin too.

Still keeping the Webbing Blade gripped in his fist, he lurched forwards and accepted the man's handshake. "Yeah," Lou just about got out, "how did you know?"

The sailor's smirk widened. "Well, brother, your friend right here, she just announced you as an ice mage, and that right there," he said, jabbing his finger at the Webbing Blade—which Lou had been so sure he'd kept concealed with his cloak, but obviously not well enough—"that's what gave you away."

"What d'you know about Auch'ray?" Lou said, slipping his hand out from the man's, and tentatively replacing the Webbing Blade back in its sheath, but not removing his fingers from the handle.

The sailor shrugged. "All about the Webbing Cloak, if you wanted to know."

Lou felt his chest tighten and an extreme chill cut right through his blood. That sensation that he'd learned to recognise as a warning of impending danger. And he would ignore it at his peril.

But before Lou could probe him for more answers, the sailor lolled back on his heels, stuck his thumbs beneath his belt and said, "Name's Captain Lunthard, brother."

"Lunthard?"

"That's the one."

Lou glanced to the barman, who was busily slicing away at their chicken breast behind the bar, but also obviously cocking his head in their direction and trying to overhear as much as he possibly could.

He wondered if there was a note of warning in the barman's gaze. He guessed it was better to be safe than sorry. It was better if he was cool with this guy, didn't go into too much detail about what they were after.

But, then again, hadn't Syre just spilled to the whole bar listening just what they were after, and what they were?

And the sailor had already mentioned the Webbing Cloak.

He guessed the time for subtlety had pretty much flown.

"Lookie here, brother," Lunthard said. "If you're real serious about trekking all the way over to the, uh"—he lowered his voice —"Threaded Pit, then I suppose it's my duty to inform you that you'll find precisely *no one* willing to take you off there."

"Because of the legends?" Lou said.

Lunthard snapped his fingers and grinned. "Precisely, brother."

Lou glanced to Syre again, and for a second he was sure that he saw that darkness swirling away, that blackness, as inky-black as her hair, right inside of her eyes. He had to take note of that, of when the dark magic might take its chance, and swipe its way through her. He was determined that *he* wouldn't be the one to allow her to be lost to her magic.

Not in the same way the Spider Warrior Auch'ray had told him about had been lost.

The two bowls of sliced chicken breast arrived before them, both the bowls making a neat *tinkle* as they landed on the counter before them. Sniffing up that scent of the roasted chicken caused Lou's gut to clench something horrible. And his mouth seemed to have all but dried up completely.

"Let me lay out a deal for you folks, how about it?" Lunthard said.

Comparing the crispy coating of Lou's chicken with Lunthard's slick, dark-toned, sweaty skin just about sealed the deal on Lou's lost appetite.

Lunthard continued, "I'm the only sailor you'll find in this here bar, brother, *hell*, that you'll find in the whole'a Irmlesbrook that's willing to ship out there. As for me, I don't care much for all that mythology hokum, oh sure, I believe in magic when I see it, but that aside, I couldn't give two cat's testicles for those stories." He leaned in closer, and Lou caught the thick stench of sour ale on his breath. "For just the right price, brother, I'll ship the both of you out to those rocks, drop anchor and wait my time for you." His eyes danced between Lou and Syre. "How's about it?"

It almost felt like Lou had arrived back on the boat, the way the room seemed to be bending about him, and his gut churning away. But he knew, from the reaction they'd just observed here in the tavern, how those sailors had reacted to even the mention of the name of the Threaded Pit that they'd have a real tough time finding another boat to charter.

All the same, he slipped Syre a quick glance before he turned back to Lunthard and said, "Fine, how much you charge?"

6

A SCULLY CRAFT

T HE NEXT MORNING was grey with fog, thick and swilling in the windless air that hung about Brinder Island. That wasn't a problem for Lou, though, since the fog meant the morning sun was rendered a faint ball of light vaguely above their heads. And so he found himself able to shuck the hood of his cloak and allow what weakened sunrays passed through the fog to lap against his skin.

Still, though, he felt that throb in his blood as the sunrays jabbed at his skin, and the frothing of his blood as his ice magic did combat with the warmth.

With Syre alongside, Lou trudged through the spindly, crooked alleyways of Irmlesbrook, following the slope of the cobblestones downwards in the direction of the port. It almost seemed too soon, to Lou, for them to be setting sail once again, headed back out onto the nauseating waves of the sea.

But the sooner he could get his hands on the Webbing Cloak, the sooner they could get back off Brinder, and Lou could put into place his plans never again to so much as look at a boat. At least not till he got a better hang of his magic, and learned ways of protecting against the more unpleasant aspects of voyaging by sea.

Already Lou could hear the *caw-caw* of the seagulls out ahead of them, and could smell that stale, salty stench of the sea. The sea breeze brushed up against his cheeks, tickling him and chilling in equal measure with the spray it carried.

That morning they'd been served a hearty breakfast at their lodgings and Lou could still taste the bacon sopping over his tongue and the insides of his cheeks. He guessed that, wherever they were headed—whatever the Threaded Pit was—he'd need that sustenance inside of him.

He had no way of knowing just how big the place was, or even a vague notion of where he had to look. Since the Webbing Cloak had been hidden there by Auch'ray, he supposed that it must be well concealed, though he hoped it would be easy.

As they descended to the port, the sound of the seagulls got louder still, and the stomach-deep crunches of their boots on the cobblestones were replaced by the squealing and groaning wooden boards of the dock beneath their feet.

And the salty stench of the air got thicker, and that nausea seemed to swill up from Lou's stomach, and that bacon threatened to make a reappearance, but, thankfully, right then, Syre thought to speak and it seemed to take his mind of those unpleasant sensations.

"There! Look!" she said, pointing out to something way off along the dock.

Lou swallowed once hard and willed his feet to stop their quivering and his brain to stop flexing and unflexing inside of his skull as if it was a bicep. He looked to where she pointed.

There, right at the end of the dock, he noticed a small-looking vessel, perhaps with no bigger capacity than for three or four people. And it had a sad, lagging sail dangling down off its mast, that looked well-fouled by guano. Standing in the base of the boat, yanking a frayed and knotted rope through his hands, stood the figure that Lou recognised as Lunthard from the *Peddy Nickle* the night before.

Their captain.

Syre quickened her pace, and Lou, hanging back for just a moment, carried on after her.

Instinctively, he reached down for the handle of the Webbing Blade, felt that all-too familiar shudder of ice magic pass through it into his fingertips. He had the Webbing Bow strapped to his back too, beneath his cloak, of course, though he doubted it would be of much use in the Threaded Pit.

Though he had no reason not to trust the kindly old woman who managed their lodgings, it was better not to leave something so valuable just lying around for anybody to take. Because he had no way of knowing how many ships sailed out of Irmlesbrook everyday, and if he returned to their lodgings to find the Webbing Bow gone then he would have zero chance of tracking it down later.

No matter how heroically he'd pursue it.

As Lou headed after Syre, he noticed how the wooden planks of the dock, beneath his feet, grew more scabbed with guano, more splintered. And several times he noticed gaping holes, large enough for his entire leg to slip down through, and the bustling harbour seawater churning away several feet below.

There was one thing about being near the water, other than the nausea, that had a real habit of phasing him:

He couldn't swim.

Though neither could Syre, it didn't seem like she shared his same fear as she skittered onwards, the planks squealing out beneath her feet as she tottered along, and he couldn't help observing that their two attitudes to the sea were worlds apart.

Syre slowed as she drew closer to Lunthard and the boat waiting for them there, bobbing gently up against the dock, as it rose and fell with the swell of the sea. When she glanced back over her shoulder, Lou thought she did it more out of remembering that *he* was the one that was supposed to be keeping her safe than out of any fear for Lunthard.

Lou did his best to ward off those relentless shreds of nausea and marched on harder, finally coming up level with her, and then the two of them walking the final few paces to where Lunthard stood up in the base of the boat.

Lunthard gave them a shrill smile as he looked over their faces. Lou could see that he had dark bags sitting beneath his eyes and his cheeks seemed to sag like stressed leather. Soon after they'd chartered his ship, Lou had taken himself and Syre back off to their lodgings to get a good night's sleep. He guessed that Lunthard had stayed at the tavern for a few more drinks before going back to his home.

If he'd gone back at all.

"Mornin', brother," Lunthard said, and then glanced back over his shoulder, his mouth and eyes screwed up. "Pity about this here fog, but nothing much to be done about that."

"Will we have to postpone?" Lou said.

Lunthard cast his gaze back in his direction, his eyes lingering over Lou's. "Nah, I grew up on Brinder, brother, know my way about these waters better than, well, I'd say pretty much any other captain you might find here."

Looking over the ship now, Lou realised that he might've made a real beginner's error when he'd chartered it without so much as having a chance to look it over. The thing looked rickety all over, its wood just as splintered as the planks of the dock and the sail even more ragged, the mast even more plastered with guano, than he'd previously thought.

And, he noticed with a lurch of the gut, there were at least half a dozen holes in the sides, and, he noticed with a further lurch of the gut, that there was a large wooden bucket in the base of the boat, all ready for bailing out.

Perhaps they might be better off finding someone else, even though Lunthard had claimed no other captain would be prepared to sail them out to the rocks. And then there was the matter of how Lunthard knew about Auch'ray, that he'd apparently shipped Auch'ray out here too. And that settled his gut for the time being, though the state of the ship still played on his mind.

"You look a little glum-faced, brother," Lunthard said. "Havin' second thoughts about headin' out to the Threaded Pit, are we?"

Lou crunched his teeth together and looked Lunthard back in the eye. "No, I was just a little worried about the state of that boat of yours."

Lunthard's smile slackened just a little. He dropped the rope he held in his hands at his feet, and then gave the ship a good slap on its side. "This here's my scully craft, this is, brother. Right made for rough and ready work, and you'd not want anything bigger for sailin' out to the Threaded Pit. And I'd certainly not take one of my bigger ships out through those rocks, brother." His smile returned to its full force. "I might know these waters better than anyone but I'm not about to plough one of my good boats through them rocks." He rested his hand in the pit of his chin. "Not even if you've got more money behind you. Makes no sense, brother."

Lou thought over Lunthard's logic and decided that he was probably right. What else were they supposed to do other than follow local advice? This was one of those situations where he just had to listen to what someone with greater expertise than he had had to say.

But, more than anything, if Auch'ray had put his trust in this captain, then he saw no reason that he shouldn't. Not only was Auch'ray a greater mage than Lou was—a *far* greater mage—but he was also several shades wiser.

Lou made no bones about admitting that.

"We okay here?" Lunthard said, his eyes moving between the two of them.

Lou glanced to Syre, who looked wide eyed with excitement at this latest sea-faring trip, and Lou had to admit to himself that, having been raised on the same sea-less plains as she had been, and despite all his wheedling nausea at the prospect, he too was a little excited to be setting out on the sea again.

"Yeah," Lou said, replying to Lunthard's question.

Lunthard smiled even wider, if that was even possible, and then crouched down for the bucket in the centre of the base of the boat, and held it out to them. "Who's bailin' out first, then, brother?"

7

AWASH IN THE WATERS OF BRINDER

THE FOG GOT THICKER, if anything, as they headed further out to sea. Lou had decided to take on the mantle of bailing out the boat to start with, and he found it pretty hard and alarming work.

Hard because the boat shifted about constantly on the surface of the waves, and he was constantly swaying about, almost losing his balance each time he crouched down.

And alarming because of the seeming constant flow of water leaking in through those holes in the sides of the ship.

Soon after they'd got on board, Lunthard had pointed out the almost totally peeled white paint on the side of the scully craft, the ship's name: the *Heredimes*, apparently, though several letters were so peeled that they could've been attempting to make out other letters.

Lou felt the gentle sting of the salt water as it lapped against his skin. It seemed to have the opposite effect on him that water usually had. Whereas he was used to there being some kind of a calming effect at having smooth, gentle, *fresh* water roll up against his skin, with the seawater it was akin to having something trying to scrub him *dry*.

The sea about Brinder was nice and clam—*flat*—as Lou listened out to the lapping of the waves against the side of the *Heredimes*. Not that it was calm for him, as he strained himself over for what seemed like the umpteenth time to swipe up more water in his pail before dumping it over the side.

As Lou stood up to take a rest, his heart beating hard, and the sweat—despite the chilly day—dribbling down his face, he took in Lunthard, standing at the tiller, eyes narrowed, and steering them along.

Lou remarked that while Lunthard was steering the ship there was no sign of that joviality he'd shown back in the tavern the night before, or even at the dock that morning. While they were out here, on the sea, he seemed totally focussed on the job at hand —deeply serious about his work.

And Lou was glad.

It gave him a little more confidence.

Almost allowed him to *trust* in Lunthard.

The fog waned as the morning went on, though it was replaced by looming dark-bottomed clouds that rolled in over their heads. Lou glanced up at them, already thinking about the possibility of a storm, and the *Heredimes's* potential resistance to that storm.

Why, it wouldn't take all that much to knock it over, to crush it into firewood. And Lou had better hope that he grabbed a hold of a good, chunky piece, otherwise he would be dragged down to the depths of the ocean.

As Lou tossed out another pail of water from the base of the boat, he looked back to where they'd come from. There was only the faintest trace of Brinder out there on the horizon, a light purple-coloured smudge. It would be a long way back if they had to return to port suddenly.

Over the course of the next few minutes, Lou felt the wind picking up, beginning to lash his cheeks rather than massage them, and he felt the ice magic within his veins pumping harder, and his heart struggling to keep up.

His mouth tasted dry and the fruit juice as well as the bacon from that morning's breakfast was a distant memory now. As the wind blew, he only caught the salt in his nostrils and at the back of his throat, and once more Lou's mind turned to the strangeness of being out here, in the middle of the sea, and he resigned himself to always being a plainsperson, for as long as he lived, if necessary.

The wind drove into the *Heredimes's* dirtied sail, billowing it out, and Lou watched as their hull cut through the rising, swelling waves. When he glanced to Lunthard, he saw that a few wrinkles had formed on the man's forehead and about his eyes, and he knew that he was concentrating hard to keep them from whatever rocks might lurk beneath the thrashing waves.

Once, as Lou was again bailing out the boat, the wind caught his cloak and, just like the sail billowing out above him, almost threatened to toss him into the waiting sea. Lou marvelled at his sudden turn of balance, the way that he'd somehow managed to keep himself from toppling out, only to look over his shoulder and see Lunthard grasping the back of his cloak—the only thing standing between Lou and a dip in the sea.

"Better if you sit now, brother!" Lunthard said, shouting above the gale in his gravelly voice.

Lou did as he said, his legs bowing out beneath him and allowing his backside to fall down onto the rickety planks of the *Heredimes*, where he sat opposite Syre, who was already buried in her own cloak, her knees tucked up to her chest, and her inky black hair all tussled up in the wind.

Lou had no way of measuring time now that the day had darkened to appear to be almost the cusp of twilight. He couldn't make out the position of the sun in the sky any longer, though he knew at the same time that he was grateful not to have to suffer the sunrays at the same time that he had to suffer this poor weather.

Spray rose up off the waves, and fizzed through the air. It settled on his skin, and there was no point in wiping it off with the material of his cloak given that his cloak was just as damp as anything else.

As they dipped down with the wave, Lou felt his stomach clenching tight once more, and a tingle run up his spine, because he knew what would follow.

The boat swept back up the other side, to the brink, and then down again.

Soon enough Lou found himself wishing that he and Syre were back on the ship that had brought them to Brinder in the first place. Because the movement of that ship had been nothing compared to this scully craft they found themselves in now.

Lou found that he had almost totally disregarded the puddle of water in the base of the boat. Because it was now a lake beneath them. And the bucket with which he'd been bailing them out now clattered against the side of the boat, only the frayed rope that tied it down keeping it from skittering over the side and into the thrashing sea.

Lou had his eyes tight shut when he heard the words on the wind or, at least, he was sure that he heard words on the wind. He concentrated hard. *Forced* himself to concentrate. And when he built up the courage to glance back over his shoulder, he realised that it was Lunthard who was calling out to them. Over the rushing sounds of the building storm.

"Thar!" he said, bellowing at the tops of his lungs while leaning forwards but keeping both his hands fixed on the tiller. "Thar!"

Lou followed the tip of Lunthard's nose, traced it out into the brewing, simmering darkened sky, and looked out over the curling and sputtering waves.

And he saw them.

The rocks.

The Threaded Pit.

8

DRY LAND, OF A KIND

LOU STARED HARDER AND HARDER, almost unbelieving of what he could see with his two eyes. But, yes, it was there. He *could* see it. Rocks rising up out of the sea, cutting up through the stormy air. *Large* rocks.

If it hadn't been so dark then he might've seen them for what they were, just a pair of small mounds growing out from the sea. But, as it was, with the whipping and churning storm all about them, they seemed large enough to be an island.

A *whole* island.

Springing up in the middle of the thrashing sea.

The salt the gale carried was like a whip against Lou's face now, and he could barely open his eyes to more than slits to see out before them, to see out into the gloom. But he could tell, from how the *Heredimes* ducked and weaved, how Lunthard scrabbled for the tiller, trying almost in vain to keep their course, that they were headed for those rocks.

And there wasn't much more he could do now other than hold on tight.

An almighty *scrape* ripped through the air, and quivered through the base of the boat. Still with his eyes clasped shut, Lou felt his heart beat its way up his throat, and throb there hard, almost as if it might choke him.

He could taste blood in his mouth, and smell it thick in his nostrils, he was sure of it. And the salt only compounded both senses, made him believe it all the more.

They were doomed.

Only when Lou waited for that swill of the wave, of that final and mighty wave, which would come to topple them over for the very last time, to tip them out into the sea to be smashed over and over until they resigned themselves to being drowned, and it didn't come, did he think to open his eyes.

All round him the wind billowed in. The sail, over their heads, continued to lash about against its mast. And then he saw that it had been furled up, that Lunthard had furled it up. Next thing, he saw Lunthard ahead of them, grasping hold of the hull of the ship, and dragging them up the beach.

Because this was a beach.

Sea-streaked pebbles lay all about them.

They glinted with the faint half-light of the storm-ridden day.

Only then did Lou think to act, and he scrabbled up from his place in the base of the boat, his legs almost totally lost to numbness and that bloody scent ripe in his nostrils, almost smothering his tongue against the base of his mouth.

He was barely aware as he leaped out of the boat, brushing

Syre's cloak as she remained there huddled against the side, and then landed in the waves lapping at the shore.

He grabbed a hold of the hull of the boat from the other side and, along with Lunthard, he drew the boat back up onto the shore, onto those pebbles. He could hear the *scrape* above even the gale and the lashing of the waves.

Only when they'd got the boat to safety, up onto the shore and away from the mottled sea, did he dare look about again.

He took in the waves, riding high, seemingly all around them, curling up with white tops as they smashed into unseen obstacles hidden by the water. Then he started to appreciate Lunthard's skill in getting them here, in bringing them to their destination. Because surely they'd arrived where they'd intended?

Just to be sure, Lou turned on his heel, looked off back at the shore, and then to a cave which lurked behind them. Though the day was not bright, Lou knew that even if they'd arrived at midday, on the calmest day of the year, he'd have had trouble seeing into the blackness of that cave.

Of the Threaded Pit.

With the gale coming in at them stronger than ever, and words all but useless now, Lou studied Lunthard's actions, and then followed.

First they helped Syre out of the boat and then turned the *Heredimes* upside down. Lou felt his muscles all tighten into knots with the almost impossible weight. Because what had seemed, back at the dock, to just be a tiny—*tiny*—craft had suddenly got heavy on them.

And after they'd completed their task, Lou allowed himself to drop down onto the beach, onto those pebbles beneath him. And though they jabbed up into his backside, he was pleased that at least they were stable. At least he was back on stable ground once again, if not for long.

He jabbed his tongue over his lips, attempting to get a little more moisture back into them, but failed since his mouth seemed just as dry as the rest of his skin. Though, at the same time, he knew that his clothes were soaked and that he was covered in seawater.

That bloody taste in his mouth hadn't gone away either, and Lou stuck a finger into his mouth expecting to come away with a crimson smear of blood, but found nothing.

No, as he turned his head he was certain that the stench of blood came from this place, this place that they'd arrived. From the mouth of the Threaded Pit looming large behind them.

An idea struck Lou and he leaned over Lunthard to speak in his ear. "Why don't we go and take refuge in the cave? It looks drier there!"

At first Lou wasn't sure he'd read Lunthard's expression right. He thought for a moment that perhaps his words had got twisted in the wind and Lunthard had understood them as a joke, because Lunthard screwed up his mouth in a grin and shook his head. The mystery wasn't put to bed till Lunthard leaned back into him and spoke.

"Nah, brother, this is as far as I go. Once you're inside that place I'm goin' in under my boat, gonna take shelter under there." He nodded to Syre, sitting on the other side of Lou. "If you like your sis there can stay with me too. If you'd prefer it."

Lou thought about this for a moment, then looked to Syre.

She hadn't moved out of that pose she'd struck back in the boat, what with how she sat on the pebble beach with her knees tucked up to her chest, and her head squeezed in there between her kneecaps.

Lou turned back to Lunthard. "What's the big issue with the cave?"

Lunthard smiled again, his long, tangled blond hair straggling into his beard, flowing all over his face. He clawed it back out of his mouth. "No one'll go in there, brother, I'm sorry to say. And you ain't gonna get me goin' there neither."

"Why's that?"

"Cursed placed, brother. Like I said, you were lucky to so much as find someone willin' to bring you out here in the first place. But I'll go no further than this here beach."

Lou looked back over to the cave, to the crooked rocks which ran up the sides of it, and the impossible blackness within. As he turned back to Lunthard, ready to ask a follow-up question, the question ripe on his lips, he couldn't get it out before Lunthard spoke again.

"Say it's cursed as those who go in thar don't return."

"So why'd you agree to bring me out here?"

Lunthard shrugged, no trace of a smile on his lips any longer, and a steely gaze crossing his eyeballs. "You're a mage, brother, figured you knew just what you were up to."

Lou looked away from him and back to the mouth of the cave once again, and then he said, so quietly as to almost be to himself, "Sometimes I'm not sure what I'm up to at all."

Lou tried to speak with Syre, but she'd pretty much shut up into herself. Fearing for the worst, he managed to unclamp that tight grip she held her head in with her knees. He wanted to see her eyes. To be sure. He forced her to open her eyes and saw that they were normal.

Not inked out in black like they had been out on the plains.

When she'd saved them all.

He turned to Lunthard. "You'll take care of her?"

"Aye, brother, won't be a problem."

Lou felt a lump stick in his throat, and then he looked on to the cave.

A little way, way out across the sea, he could see a glimmer of sunlight breaking through the gloomy clouds above. Soon he knew that the sun would be shining down once more. And it would begin to affect him again.

And his magic.

With that thought on his mind, he trod his way along the pebble beach and towards the mouth of the cave.

THE THREADED PIT

L OU KEPT HIMSELF steady as he felt the shade of the cave loom over him. The air, dank and cool. A gentle *drip-drip* off in the distance. He felt the ice magic tingling through his veins as if in response to where he was. He knew very little about this place, only that Auch'ray had told him that here was where he'd find the Webbing Cloak.

The rest was up to him.

Here, in the cave, the scent of blood got thicker in the air, and he was certain that he had cut himself, that he might have some cut in his mouth or on his arm. *Somewhere.* But when he checked he couldn't find anything.

As he proceeded further into the cave, he noticed the pebbles beneath his feet change, to be replaced by fine sand. A path, of sorts. Rocks jutted up at him on all sides and he could just about make out their positions from the glistening of condensation sparkling off them from the little light that dribbled into the cave.

Soon he wouldn't be able to see the nose in front of his face.

Now was the time for him to try out that charm he'd learned a while ago.

Back on the mountaintop with Auch'ray.

Just as Auch'ray had instructed him, Lou withdrew the Webbing Blade from its sheath. Though he could cast the charm himself, without the aid of the magical artefact, Auch'ray had made it clear to him that the magic would come more quickly—and more powerfully—with the artefact in his hand.

He also reached back for the Webbing Bow, slipped it down off his shoulder, and grasped the grip tight.

Two magical artefacts would be even more effective.

However, Lou also remembered the warnings that Auch'ray had given him, about how though these magical artefacts would make his magic much thicker—*much* stronger—and easier to summon, it would also place Lou in much greater danger if he didn't take care.

And if Lou allowed the magic to take him over then he would become lost to it—lost to the ice portion of the magical field . . . just like the Spider Warrior had been, the legend that Auch'ray had told him about.

As Lou mumbled the words, he felt the hum in his chest, drawing on the magic in his veins, the *ice* magic, and bringing it into a kind of froth, that bucked and bubbled up. He shut his eyes tight and felt it all flowing to his solar plexus, his mind, his lips muttering the words, becoming like secondary elements to the magic passing through him now.

And then, just as Auch'ray had instructed him, Lou allowed the magic to all well up inside, and then he let it go.

A frosty blue glow burst out before him. A clustered ball of energy. He watched it swirl in the air before him for a few seconds, revolving around, brought into being between his two magical artefacts. And then, shouldering the Webbing Bow, and holding the Webbing Blade down at his thigh, he looked off into the distance, to where the shadows scurried away from the light.

As Lou wandered on through the cave, he felt the floor beneath his feet sloping away, diving down. In his mind, he imagined himself plunging beneath the level of the waves. That thought stopped him briefly as he thought about what might happen if the waves surged in through the mouth of the cave. It would hurl him down here.

Drown him.

But he stopped those thoughts before they took hold, because he was, after all, Louson Dorf: Ice Mage, and no longer Lou the Frightened and Feeble Working Hand.

He had to be brave now. He had come all the way out here to claim the third and final ice magic artefact and once he obtained it, it would have no mercy on him. There would be no time for fear.

Not if he wished to survive.

Off in the distance, ahead of him, he continued to hear that *drip-drip* sound, and the bloody stench got even thicker in the air. But it was also dank and musky, as if soured by the sea breeze that must've wafted in here for years and years. He could almost taste the blood on his tongue when he opened his mouth to gulp at the air—the thinning air, or the air which seemed to thin as he dropped deeper below the waves.

There was a chill, too, which swamped in at his heels, and sent a tingle running up his spine. What was it that someone had once told him? About how, as an ice mage, the shadows and the night-time were his? The shadows were his? It had been Hildie, hadn't it?

Hildie.

A long time since he had seen her.

He wondered where she was now.

Deeper down, further on in the cave, in the tunnel ahead, he heard a loud *thud*, followed by an odd pattering sound.

Lou grabbed the Webbing Blade tighter, held it at his chest, and with his other hand, reached back for the Webbing Bow.

His heart ticked on as he stood prone, ready and waiting for whatever it was, out there in the gloom. He stared as hard as he could to the limit of his illumination charm, to the edge of its field of frosty blue light. But saw nothing but scurrying shadows.

Until he saw the sparkle of seemingly a thousand eyes.

10

SPIDER

LOU'S HANDS worked much quicker than his brain. He snapped out of his daze, and fitted an arrow to the string of the Webbing Bow, lined it up, then let it fly.

The arrow speared through the air and caught its target.

A guttural *hiss* flurried through the air.

Lou got a look at his adversary.

A spider. An enormous spider. At least three times his height and more than five or six times his width.

His heart stuck in his throat, but, again, his hands worked to notch another arrow, and then let fly.

With great thick hairy legs, and a constantly chewing jaw.

Fangs speckled with what appeared to be dried blood.

It thrashed wildly at where the arrow had struck—in what Lou guessed to be its forehead ... if spiders *had* foreheads.

Lou let fly another. Then another. Another still.

Then he waited, his chest bringing the front of his cloak up and down as he strained to gulp in every last lungful of air he could in this dank and steel-smelling place.

The spider's legs and jaws thrashed. White foamed rushed from its mouth. And its eyes all got caught into a tremble.

Lou gritted his teeth and lined up another arrow, what would be the killing arrow. But, standing with his arm arched back, ready to let fly again, he realised that it wouldn't be necessary.

The spider was dead.

It rolled over onto its side, its legs all crunched up to its belly, and then became still.

Lou only realised he was holding his breath when he felt his lungs burn from the effort. He let go, and then stared long and hard at the spider, thinking about how this creature was so much like its innocuous, smaller cousins.

He waited out the time, waiting for longer and longer, with each passing second feeling his legs locking up all the more. And he knew that if he didn't move soon, if he didn't go to pass the fallen spider, then he would never advance into the Threaded Pit.

He would *never* find the Webbing Cloak.

And so, allowing the Webbing Bow to lower in his grip, but not letting *one* muscle relax as he still held back the string, he slipped by the dead spider, and deeper into the cave.

Once the adrenalin had seeped out of Lou's system, and he'd done his best to forget about the spider he had killed . . . or at least to force himself *not* to think about it, he slung the Webbing Bow back over his shoulder and then turned his mind to his illumination charm.

It was strong, and the light even, steady.

He was proud of how well he'd summoned it, all things considered.

Perhaps he wasn't a complete and total failure of a mage after all.

But there was still time.

The tunnel got more and more narrow as he proceeded, and as his heart returned to its normal rhythms, and the dank, musky air grew familiar to him—even the bloody stench losing its edge—he noticed a few of the spider webs which hung from the walls. What had once been the fallen spider's nest . . . or what he used to catch his prey.

Lou had just got to wondering what things the spider preyed on when he got his answer.

Before him, wrapped up in a silky wcb on the floor of the cave, was a human skull.

He guessed that the sailors had a little more sense in fearing this place than he'd given them credit for. If he hadn't been in possession of his magical powers then he never would've dared set foot in this place. If he'd been a mortal he'd have been dead by now.

But, then again, if he'd truly been a mortal then he wouldn't have been here at all.

Lou had no way of telling the time he had been down in the Threaded Pit. It seemed, from the state of his aching muscles, and the lack of air, that he must've been walking for hours and hours. But he'd have had no way of knowing if he'd been walking for days. The illumination charm, with its even—almost *sickly*—light had a habit of stripping his memory of all natural light. It kept him awake . . . kept him *alert*.

And he made sure to pay attention for any other beasties that might be hanging about the Threaded Pit.

As he went on, he took care to keep track of any more of the spider webs, any more of the human bones down here. And he noted there were none, hadn't been any for what seemed like hours ago. He thought about how the spider most likely had stayed up closer to the mouth of the cave, only to rush out onto the beach and drag shipwrecked sailors down into its cave . . . into the Threaded Pit . . . before devouring them.

Yes, that made sense to Lou.

But that also begged the question of just how far this cave went on for.

And how much further he had to go before he found what he was seeking.

Lou's illumination charm had begun to dim when he started to hear the echo of his footsteps, coming from up ahead. He guessed that, perhaps, he was about to come across a chamber, a large space which echoed all his sounds about itself.

That sounded like something that Auch'ray would deem to be grand enough to house the Webbing Cloak.

Lou carried on his way, now straining his eyes against the dimming light of his charm, and trying to see ahead. He knew that he would need to cast another charm soon, but he would put it off as long as he could.

The conjuring was draining and he hadn't the patience to stop and sleep. For one, he had no idea of what else there might be lurking in the dark. And, for another, he had no intention of dozing off and not getting back to the shore in time to hitch a ride back on the boat with his sis and Lunthard.

He had no real way of knowing how long Lunthard would wait before giving up hope on him, though he hadn't yet paid him, that was *something* at least.

As Lou drew closer to this forthcoming echo chamber, he realised that the colour of his illumination charm was changing as he proceeded. Changing right before his eyes. At first, Lou was certain that it was just a trick of the light, that his brain was beginning to hallucinate from the lack of oxygen, and the dank smell of blood everywhere. But no, he was certain. The light coming off his illumination charm had taken on a tangerine tinge. And the tangerine tinge was getting brighter.

For a giddy moment, Lou thought that perhaps he had travelled right through the centre of the Earth, and ended up on the other side of the planet.

Was this the sun peeping out from within?

. . . No, that was a ridiculous notion.

More likely, he had been headed up a slope somewhere. That was more likely. He no longer had a real reference of whether he was going up or down.

Lou kept on moving along the tunnel, the light getting brighter. As he got closer, Lou realised that the light coming from ahead was flickering.

Firelight?

Down here, beneath the sea?

It sounded ridiculous.

But, as Lou made his way onwards, and he headed on through the doorway, he saw that it was firelight.

An enormous great chamber opened out before him. It was all dug out of rock. A space at least as big as four or five houses.

Lou instinctively reached for the handle of the Webbing Blade.

Torches hung down from the walls, each of them with a flame flickering away. And, as Lou well knew, for there to be fire down here, so far beneath the sea, there must've been someone to light it.

Or else a mage—an *extremely* strong mage—had summoned ever-lasting flames.

And the first mage Lou thought of, the only one that he could imagine being capable of such a thing, was Ma'reygar.

If Ma'reygar had been down here, if he had already taken the Webbing Cloak, then Lou might as well turn around right now. Because this would've been a wasted journey. And it was beyond belief that someone like *him* would be able to wrestle away something that Ma'reygar wanted.

Especially something as important as the Webbing Cloak.

Lou glanced about the chamber, and examined the torches that hung off the walls. He could feel his chest twitching, and the ice magic running through his blood. Something inside of him was telling him to run. But he wouldn't run. If he wanted to be a mage—a *real* mage—then he needed to stand and fight.

And so, with that thought etched on his mind, he slid the Webbing Blade out from its sheath, and tightened his grip on its handle.

Lou completed his examination of the chamber quickly and efficiently, and realised that this was a dead end. Or, at least, this was where the trail ran cold. He had reached the very bottom of the Threaded Pit.

Once this dawned on Lou, he did another tour of the chamber, checking to see if he'd missed something. Perhaps Auch'ray had put a hidden doorway into the place, but when Lou went round all the walls, tapping away, trying to find a hollow spot, he came up empty handed.

Tired from the long walk, and feeling the flickering flames begin to cause his skin to break out into tiny little pimples all over . . . the ice magic reacting against the warmth, he decided that he should just get it over with, that he should summon up another illumination charm and make his way back out to the mouth of the cave.

As he stretched long and hard, his back feeling a little stiff from all the constant travelling he'd been doing—it felt like he'd constantly been on his feet ever since leaving the encampments. Travelling the whole time. Soon, though, he would be back among his people, and he would be able to protect them.

Perhaps having only the Webbing Blade and the Webbing Bow would be sufficient.

Lou turned to look at the doorway, the way that he had entered into this underground chamber and he saw a figure standing there. At first he couldn't believe his eyes. But then he was sure. *Certain.* And he slung the Webbing Bow off his shoulder and notched an arrow, ready to take the pre-emptive strike.

He might not get another chance.

11

A WANDERING PRISONER

LOU DIDN'T KNOW why he didn't let fly his arrow straight away. Perhaps it was because he had some nagging feeling at the back of his mind, a narrow possibility—nothing more—that this figure might be either Lunthard or Syre. He had some wild notion that they might've wandered down here, all the way, after him.

In the dark.

It *was* a pretty wild notion.

And, after a long moment, Lou still didn't let go of his arrow, because the figure made no movement towards him. In fact, he only stood there, in the doorway, looking back at Lou, remaining a silhouette to him.

"Who's there?" Lou called out.

The silhouette just continued to regard him.

Lou's mind wheeled back to the first time he'd seen Hildie. Way back when she'd come to him as a hobblesman, back out there on the plains, when they'd been fleeing Endmere, burned to the ground by her . . . and then she'd warned them of the cursed bears that had soon come bounding out of the darkness.

Was she here now?

Had she somehow followed him?

If so, then he should shoot her. *Kill* her before she killed him. Or got the chance to kill someone else.

The figure just remained in the doorway, apparently not inclined to move whatsoever, and Lou waited for the figure to move from his—*her?*—place.

And then, just as Lou felt the string of his bow begin to grow impossibly taut in his fingers, for his finger to ready to release the arrow, the figure spoke.

"My name is Xeda."

Lou's heart welled up into his throat. He just caught his finger, allowed the string to go slack again, and he dropped the Webbing Bow down to his side. Every nerve in his body seemed to tingle, and those torches shedding light over the chamber caused sweat to prickle out from his pores. And that dank, bloody odour came back to him.

He tasted it in his mouth.

Could almost hear blood dripping somewhere off up the tunnel.

Or was it just the condensation from the sea air?

Lou continued to glare at the figure standing in the doorway. "*What* did you say?"

The figure remained there, apparently not willing to say that much. And, in any case, Lou had heard him just fine the first time. He just didn't believe what he had said.

He felt the feeling slowly come back to his hands, and he allowed the string of the Webbing Bow to go completely slack, but he still kept the end of the arrow entwined in his fingers, ready to bring it up at a moment's notice.

"Those used to be mine," the figure—Xeda?—said.

Lou felt that same daze drift over him, and he looked about himself. To the Webbing Bow in his hands, and then to the Webbing Blade at his side. Yes, that would be just what Xeda would've said. He was the Spider Warrior, after all . . . or as Auch'ray had told him.

But that couldn't be right, because Xeda was . . . was *dead*.

And that meant that Lou was seeing ghosts.

Or perhaps a very good illusion, an illusion that Auch'ray hadn't seen fit to tell Lou even existed, let alone teach him it. Maybe this was just a test. *Another* test.

"May I prowl a little closer without fear of reproach?" Xeda said.

The way that Xeda spoke was odd, an extremely old-style of speech, as if he had learned to talk out of books . . . like the books that the teacher used to read back when Lou had been in school.

Lou's tongue felt like a throbbing unwieldy mess, but he managed to get out a simple, "Yes."

Xeda hung back in that doorway for a few more seconds before making a move.

Lou understood why Xeda had said 'prowl' because that was just how he walked. He walked with a prowl, as if he was stalking something. And he stuck to the shadows of the chamber, never once emerging into the light from the torches.

What was that Auch'ray had said to him about how Xeda had chosen not to walk with weakness? To exile it from his mind? Hadn't that been what had caused his downfall, what had led Ma'reygar to ultimately destroy him?

Xeda drew closer still and Lou got the chance to see his face in the flicker of the torchlight. His skin was so pale as almost to be light blue in tone, and his eyes were wild, constantly bobbing about their sockets, adjusting, prying over him, part by part.

It made Lou feel greatly uncomfortable, made his skin prickle all over.

Xeda wore a cloak, much like Lou's, black and with missing patches, a thread hanging off here and there. Xeda drew to a halt when he reached the edge of the glow of the torchlight. He tilted his head back and sniffed hard at the air, like an animal, Lou thought.

Then, all of a sudden, Xeda snapped his head back to lock his eyes with Lou's. "You had no trouble with Fyutior?"

"Fyutior?" Lou said, without thinking, just tracing the word he'd heard with his lips and tongue.

Xeda flared his eyes and a twitch seemed to shimmy down his body, starting at his shoulders and finishing at his hips. "The spider," he said.

"Ah," Lou said. "No, I killed it."

Xeda's eyes rounded and Lou noticed him stick out his lower lip in a pout, and then, without warning, tears filled his eyes. They rolled down his cheeks in fat drops. When they reached his chin they dropped to the ground. "*Killed*?" Xeda said in a shrill, almost childlike voice.

Taken off guard by the whole act, Lou found himself backing up a couple of steps, and then sliding his hand down his side to feel for the handle of the Webbing Blade. He managed a nod while taking in the odd spectacle of Xeda, of his frail body, and tightly wrapped, pale skin.

Xeda fell down into a crouch, still remaining aware of where the shadow was, and taking care to stay out of the torchlight.

And, from where he crouched, he let loose a wild and blood-curdling scream.

The sound echoed about the chamber, and Lou, almost unconsciously, withdrew the Webbing Blade from its sheath, and held it, drawn down at his side, ready for whenever Xeda broke out and tried to attack him.

The sound, it was almost unhuman, almost like a pig's squeal as the butcher brought the blade down across its neck.

And that stench of blood in this place, that dank and musty odour, rushed back over Lou, and made his stomach clench. His fist clenched too, around the handle of the Webbing Blade.

Xeda continued to sob away.

Lou felt a tingle rush through his veins. That same warning striking his blood, and he knew he had to take extreme care. Xeda … whatever this thing was, it was fighting on its terrain, and so he had to stay aware of every aspect of his surroundings.

But, more than anything else, Lou kept his eyes fixed on Xeda, before him, expecting him to rush at him at any second, to catch Lou unaware.

Xeda shook quietly, and Lou could still hear the sob at the base of his throat, and could feel the sob shredding through the air —*humming*, almost.

Lou eyed the doorway, the way back up to the tunnel, and to the relative safety of the shore. All those tossing waves, and the terror that had struck him in the boat seemed so far away now. Because he might never leave this room if he didn't take care.

Gradually, Xeda's voice got louder, breaking out from the mumbled sobs, and forming comprehensible words—words comprehensible to Lou, in any case.

"... Down here, down, down ... down here ..."

Lou squeezed the handle of the Webbing Blade even tighter and, going against just about every impulse in his body, he took a step forwards. *Closer* to Xeda. He felt his eyes stiffen in their sockets as he didn't dare allow Xeda to leave his glare.

"Down, down, down ... down, down ... down *here*."

With the final word, Xeda snapped his neck upwards, and caught Lou in his stare. His mouth was bitter and twisted, his fingers so stiff as to appear like claws.

Lou brought the Webbing Blade round to his chest and held it there, feeling the reassuring chill coming off its blade, sending shimmers through his blood.

Xeda's eyes traced the blade, and then worked their way upwards slowly to meet Lou's. "You, you have come here for the *Webbing Cloak*."

Lou thought about denying it, but could see no basis for doing so. Anyway, he might anger Xeda, and that seemed like a poor idea considering the circumstances. "Yes," Lou said. "That's right."

Lou hadn't quite known what to expect. He supposed that he'd been expecting the attack to come then, for Xeda to try and lash at his throat, and not to stop until he had ripped Lou's heart out ... or Lou had stuck the Webbing Blade through Xeda ... though he had his doubts of its effectiveness given that, from what Auch'ray had told him, he knew Xeda to be an ice mage too.

... Or, at least, he *had* been an ice mage.

Tears still sparkled in Xeda's eyes, and he brought his hands up, intertwined his bony fingers and Lou listened to the *crack* of his joints. He cocked his head to one side. "Auch'ray," he said. "Auch'ray, he told you to come here."

Again, Lou thought for a moment, then decided to answer honestly. "He told me about this place, about the Webbing Cloak. But he didn't *tell* me to come here."

"Hmm."

Lou tried his best to read Xeda, to work out what he was thinking. But it was almost impossible. Xeda had so many twistings of his features, so many *tics* that he couldn't separate each. All he could do was assemble the big picture. And that told him to stay on his guard.

"Do you know where the Webbing Cloak is?" Lou said.

Xeda's eyes searched Lou's for several moments, and then his mouth twitched several times before settling on a smile. And wrinkles cracked the otherwise smooth, pale skin around his eyes. Then he made a tutting sound at the back of his throat and shook his head in a mad frenzy.

Lou squeezed the handle of the Webbing Blade tighter still.

"Auch'ray he ... he *lied* to you, didn't he, didn't he ..."

Lou realised that Xeda was waiting for him to tell him his name, and so he decided to help him out. "Louson Dorf," he said.

"Yes, Louson Dorf," Xeda said. "Auch'ray he *lied* to you. He said . . . he said that I . . . I was *dead*, didn't he? He said I was *dead*."

Lou listened to his heart hammering away in his eardrums. He felt that salty scent crawling its way up his nostrils again, and couldn't help but taste the bloodiness in the air. Everything was just so dank down here ... everything so *moist*. Though he hated the sun up above, he couldn't imagine living down here, in the Threaded Pit, in these conditions, forever.

In that moment he knew that he would have to learn to live with his weakness, to live with the fire, just like Auch'ray had instilled in him. If he couldn't learn to live with fire then he would only live a half-life . . . like the life that Xeda lived down here.

"Yes," Lou said, managing to reply. "Auch'ray said that Ma'reygar killed you—that your ice magic turned you insane and you became the Spider Warrior. You murdered innocents —mortals."

Xeda's eyes seemed to slink back in their sockets and a child-like aspect dawned over him. He clasped his hands tighter and there was another *crack* of his joints as he did so. "Mm, yes, I can believe that. I can believe that."

"But why?" Lou said. "Why did he do it?"

Xeda's lips twitched again. His smile widened. And his eyes once more strayed onto the Webbing Blade and then the Webbing Bow. "Because, because, because"—his eyes snapped back onto Lou's—"he is ashamed, ashamed, ashamed—"

"'Ashamed,' why?"

"Because he couldn't *kill* me, he didn't have the heart to *kill* me, and so he brought me here, he *left* me here, *left* me here to *die*."

"And he hid the Webbing Cloak here too?"

Xeda grinned, and all the wrinkles opened the cracks in his face once again.

Lou looked about himself, and then back down at the Webbing Blade that he held in his fist. He stared at the shimmer of the torchlight along its edge. When Lou looked up, Xeda was staring at him or, more precisely, the Webbing Blade clutched in his fist.

Xeda nodded to the Webbing Blade. "And he gave that to Ma'reygar too."

Lou felt his chest tighten, and thought about what Auch'ray had told him. Yes, though it was now clear that Auch'ray had lied to him about the death of Xeda—of the Spider Warrior—he had at least admitted the truth to Lou about having given the Webbing Blade over to Ma'reygar. At least that confirmed just what he had been told himself. And perhaps Lou could stretch himself to, if not trust Xeda, see his way to believing the version of the truth he told.

Xeda screwed up his eyes. "But I have also a question: how did you wrestle the Webbing Blade from Ma'reygar?"

"I didn't," Lou said. "It was *given* to me."

Xeda's lips thinned and he nodded slightly. Lou was sure that he heard a slight gasp at the back of Xeda's throat as he absorbed that piece of information. "Yes," he said, "for someone like you to defeat someone like Ma'reygar, it would have been impossible."

"Why didn't Ma'reygar kill you?"

Xeda's eyelids drooped down and he made an odd sniffling sound. "Because Ma'reygar and Auch'ray were friends, and for him to destroy his friend's apprentice, well, it would have been a heartless act—like destroying a part of himself."

"And so he sent you down here?"

"Hmm," Xeda said, with a nod.

Lou wondered which was more cruel, killing Xeda or having him sent down here, into the Threaded Pit to live out the rest of his days underground.

In the darkness.

Lou thought he could hear a scuttling sound off in the distance. At first he disregarded it, thought it just an aural hallucination. Some memory of that spider he'd killed—Fyutior, as Xeda had called it. He had walked a long way and was tired. This torchlight, these flames dancing on his skin, weren't helping. And he knew he had to get back out through the tunnels, and back out to Syre and Lunthard lest they give up hope for him and sail away.

Just as he turned to Xeda, ready to bid him goodbye, and to take his leave from the Threaded Pit, a failure, he caught the motion out of the corner of his eye. And could hardly believe what he saw.

What was scuttling in through the doorway.

12

SPIDERS

LOU STARED long and hard, watching them pouring through the doorway, and into the chamber. Spiders. Dozens and dozens of them. All about the size of his foot.

That dank, bloody scent got thicker in the air, and Lou felt his stomach lurch. The temperature all round Lou seemed to cool and Lou could now taste the blood inside his mouth, as if it had found its way in past his lips and now bathed his tongue in it.

His hands fumbled back over his shoulder, and he brought the Webbing Bow back round, holding it steady in his grip, and readying an arrow, picking out one of his targets then letting fly.

The arrow found its target, spearing it and freezing it dead.

Lou worked on, pushing himself to go harder and faster, to keep rattling off his arrows. He hardly had time to aim, and just worked on instinct, as he'd hoped he would soon do after he'd practised a while at archery. He popped off each of the spiders, one by one, and yet seemed to be making little inroads into them.

Because they kept on pouring in through the doorway.

Lou glanced to his side and saw Xeda there, still stuck down in his crouch, and before he had time to think he lurched forwards and snatched a hold of Xeda's frail wrist, yanked him up to his feet, and dragged him on behind him as the spiders faced up to them.

Xeda drew close to Lou, his lips almost brushing Lou's ear as he spoke. "These . . . these are her *babies*."

"What?" Lou said, releasing Xeda's hand and then taking to firing off at the spiders yet again, catching a good number of them, but not stopping the constant flow.

"Her *babies*," Xeda repeated. "They have burst out from her. When you killed her. They shall feast and grow. When there is no food they shall eat one another, till there is only one remaining. And . . . and she shall be the new mistress of the Threaded Pit."

Lou kept on firing off arrows, not appreciating Xeda's poetic reflections at this point. Each time he let an arrow loose, he felt the chill sweep over his chest, knot his muscles temporarily, and squeeze his heart.

The temperature had dropped several degrees now, and Lou could feel himself trembling uncontrollably. When he looked about himself he realised that his illumination charm had now completely collapsed, and the only light in this chamber now came from the flickering torches up on the walls.

The spiders kept on skittering closer, and Lou took several steps back, feeling himself stumble into Xeda who lurked behind him, and he knew they were headed for the wall. That soon the spiders would have them cornered. And then, just as Xeda said, they would consume them.

One of the spiders caught Lou's eye, having broken away from the main group, and now skittering ever closer. He aimed the Webbing Bow at it and let fly. And missed.

His heart skipped a few beats.

He had hardly notched another arrow into the bow before the spider leaped.

It leaped up, its legs flailing through the air, and landed on Xeda.

Lou watched on, feeling as if the world was moving in slow motion, that effect he knew to be the magic in his veins, giving him an opportunity—a *chance*. But he was too slow, and he watched on as the spider's razor-sharp fangs dug into Xeda's neck. Honey-coloured poison oozed out and met with Xeda's freshly spilled blood.

Lou fumbled the Webbing Bow again. Finally he lined up his target. He shot the spider off Xeda and watched it tumble down to the ground. He glanced briefly to Xeda's wound and then remembered the others. He watched them all, more than fifty now, surely, all black and hairy and scrabbling for him. And he knew that this was the end.

He would never fight them all off.

Xeda let loose a moan, his mouth a gaping black hole, almost as black as the entrance to the cave had been. And he staggered from one foot to the other, arms groping desperately for something to hold onto. He finally found the wall and steadied himself. He doubled over and panted. His eyes near enough bulged from their sockets.

Lou knew the end was near now. Just a few more seconds. A little more of life before the ever-lasting embrace of death.

On the periphery of his vision he watched the spiders advancing further and further, with each step from those hairy legs of theirs they drew closer. Inching further forwards. Destroying all hope of escape.

Xeda contorted his lips and moaned harder. With his back pressed up against the wall of the chamber, he slipped downwards and landed on the ground. His limbs seemed to grow out from him, unwieldy extras to his body, an unnecessary extravagance.

Lou let fly another few arrows and watched the spiders turn on their backs and die, just like the larger spider—their *mother*—had done. And then he saw the glow. The glow that seemed to emanate out from Xeda's solar plexus, and to hum lightly through the air. A light-blue glow, just like the one that he could produce when he put his mind to it.

Only when he watched it grow in intensity, saw the light spin in mid air and then grow tighter, spin harder, did Lou think to duck.

And he did.

Just in time.

Lou covered his eyes with his arm and fell backwards up against the wall of the chamber. He could feel that sting of the ice passing through the air, of Xeda unleashing his magic.

Magic that Lou had been certain he hadn't had.

The blood in Lou's veins seemed to bubble and froth, responding to this mighty outpouring, and Lou gritted his teeth hard, feeling his mind swirl at the strength of the magic. He took care to keep himself as flush with the floor as he could, so much so that he only realised the cool sensation up against his cheek was the smooth stone floor of the chamber after he'd been lying there for what seemed like hours.

That dank, bloody stench stayed thick in the air and he felt it wind up, toil up, his nostrils, attempt to burrow its way down his throat and into his lungs. But he pushed it away. Refused to let it into himself, and then, feeling the magic begin to wane, he opened his eyes and looked out around him.

Dozens of spiders. All turned over on their backs. Legs curled into their bellies.

Lou felt his muscles all tight and his blood threaten to freeze in his veins. A kind of relief swept over him, but only in numbing waves, causing him to tremble all the more. And to feel his heart stick at the base of his throat.

And only then did he realise that the chamber was now lit with that same pale blue light, the one that he had seen Xeda summoning from within himself, the spell he had cast to take care of all these dead spiders about them.

Up on the walls, the torches had been extinguished, from the magic, he supposed, and that now the only light that remained in the chamber came from the remains of the spell, still twirling about the chamber.

Lou only had time to look to Xeda, to see him lying slumped up against the wall of the chamber, his hand pressed to his neck, where the spider had bitten him, his eyes lolling about their sockets, before the light went out completely.

And they were left in total darkness.

13

THE WAY OUT

LOU FELT the darkness ebb out from the corners and swell to consume everything, to take over his entire vision, and to make the ice magic twitch within his veins. The dank, bloody odour was impossible to stand. He knew he had to get out right now. Already he was sure he could taste the salt at the back of his throat with the very thought of the shore, of emerging back out from the Threaded Pit, and escaping this place.

The spiders were all dead now.

Weren't they?

Though the gloom was complete, Lou could still hear Xeda grumbling about from where he lay. Lou knew that he had to do something to help him. He had charms that he could use to heal him. And they were all nimble upon his tongue.

He picked the first one that came to him and, reaching out to feel the wall to guide him on his way, he made his way towards the direction of Xeda's groaning.

When he almost stumbled over him, Lou began the incantations, feeling his lips trace those rote-learned phrases, the ones that he had read out of books, and the ones which Auch'ray had forced him to get right—not only to pronounce word-perfect but also to have etched in his brain.

Lou recalled the lesson Auch'ray had given him about a mage never having time in the heat of battle . . . out in the field . . . to quickly shoot off home to consult his library.

No, he had to be prepared always.

And, right now, Lou knew he was prepared.

He kneeled down at Xeda's side, feeling the strain on his knees from the hard floor beneath him. He could still hear Xeda's mumblings. He was delirious, Lou was sure, that he still believed the spiders were all around and that he had to take care of them.

But he had already fought them off.

Lou spoke through the phrases, dimly aware that Xeda's words were getting louder, and then he realised that it was a single word. Hard and consistent. Uncompromising.

"No. No. No."

Lou leaned back a little from Xeda and turned his mind back to the healing charm that he was weaving, the one, if he could only just get it right, that would save Xeda's life.

Just as Xeda had saved his.

But Xeda grew more insistent. "No, no, no. *NO!*"

The final 'no' was so abrupt and percussive, that Lou drew back from him on instinct, and he found himself losing his place in his incantations. His current stanza totally lost to his memory. He would have to start again. How could he make Xeda understand that what he was doing was for his own good?

Lou began again, only to be cut off almost right away.

"NO!" Xeda said again.

Lou made no attempt to start afresh a third time. He could

already feel the ice in his blood begin to sting him, and he knew that he was drawing on magic with dwindling energy and that soon he would have none left.

"Light, light, light," Xeda said.

"I don't understand."

"Light. Light. Light. *LIGHT!*"

And then Lou, finally, understood. He knew that Xeda was telling him that he needed to cast his illumination charm. But Lou knew he could find his way out of the Threaded Pit without it, if need be. He could find his way back along the narrow tunnel.

And he would hope he wouldn't bump into another of these spiders.

"I want to help you," Lou said, surprised how close his voice was to a whisper.

"No," Xeda said, snatching breaths. "No . . . it is . . . my time."

Lou waited a long moment and then said, "But I can get you out of here. What they've done to you . . . whatever you did before, we can speak about it."

"I have caused . . . much . . . pain and suffer . . . *suffering.*" Xeda gulped down yet more air, and in the darkness Lou pictured Xeda's chest rising and falling hard. "It is my time," he repeated.

Lou stared into the gloom for a long time, at where he knew Xeda lay just inches before his nose. He thought of the stories which Auch'ray had told him—the terrible things that he had done under the influence of his ice magic . . . how he had lost himself to the ice magic.

But, surely, now with him here, in this pitiful state, he was no danger to anyone at all.

Or was Lou being naïve?

He had been naïve with Hildie . . . though where were they right now? Did he forgive her the murder she had brought in burning those villages? Had that been balanced out in her saving the encampments from those wandering mages?

... Or could some things just never be made right?

"Light, light, light," Xeda said again, from the very pit of his throat.

Lou waited a few moments, allowed the thoughts to tick over in his mind, and he carefully took time to study each, before discarding it. And then he reached his decision.

He began to mutter the incantations for his illumination charm. The chamber seemed to bounce his voice about, all around him, coming back at him, vibrating all about his body.

Despite the pale blue light illuminating the chamber, showing all those dozens of scattered spiders' bodies lying all around them—the light reflecting the drool off their still fangs—the casting of the illumination charm only seemed to have served to incense Xeda. And his panicked mutterings grew more determined.

"Light, light, light, light, light, light!"

Lou gazed down on him, seeing him sprawling out over the floor now, his chest rising and falling rapidly with his breathing. That wound on his neck now pulsing with blood that appeared black in this light. "I . . . I've done it," Lou said. "There's light here now, there's—"

But Xeda just kept on shaking his head, vigorously, from side to side, his mouth still muttering the word, saying, "Light," over and over again. And finally Lou realised just what he wanted, what he was trying to tell him.

Xeda wanted to be brought back out through the tunnels, to go back to the shore, and to be shown the *day*light. That was what he wished for.

Lou looked round himself yet again, to all those spider corpses surrounding them, and then to the ethereal light that beamed all around this chamber of the Threaded Pit, and then he crouched down and helped Xeda up to his feet.

Xeda helped him as much as he could, and his body was as fragile as a baby bird's, his bones no heavier than kindling. In fact, Lou had no trouble in lifting him into his arms, in carrying him like an oversized, scrawny child.

And in that way, they proceeded out of the chamber, and back up that never-ending slope, headed back for the shore.

14

ESCAPED

WHEN LOU SAW the faint pink light up ahead, lighting up the pale blue sky, he was almost certain that there was a ball of flames that had burst out on the beach. One that had somehow risen out of the sea. And his first thought about it was Hildie.

And, his second, with a tremor through his heart:

Ma'reygar.

As he drew closer, though, he knew that it had nothing to do with magic whatsoever, that it was merely the sun setting. Or, as he got closer still, and noticed that there was none of that weakening of the daylight, and that the pinkish light was climbing up into the sky, he realised that this wasn't a sunset at all.

This was a sun*rise*.

He arms ached from carrying Xeda for so long now, and he could feel the muscles up his spine twitching. Now only one thought played out on his mind. He hoped and prayed that Syre and Lunthard were still there, waiting for him on the shore.

Would Lunthard have allowed them to spend the night out there on the pebble beach?

Lou's mouth too was totally dried up now. The little water he had taken with him in the canister down at his side had long run out, and he'd kept himself going for the last few hours of his climb up through the cave with the idea of getting a droplet of water— even *seawater*—onto his tongue. Just the idea almost made him go crazy.

And the dank stench of blood lifted from the air as the mouth of the cave got wider, as the rising sun got brighter, and its rays glinted off the grey—and, reassuringly—*still* waves of the sea. He breathed that familiar salty odour once again, just like he seemed to have been washed in for weeks and weeks now.

As he quickened his step, he noticed his boots come to crunching over pebbles instead of sand. He stumbled a couple of times, feeling the pebbles skitter out from beneath his feet, roll off, scraping against one another as he went.

When the first of the sun's rays cast over his skin, he felt the burning sensation there, the ice magic within his veins protesting against its contact with him, and he felt that tightening of his chest and the rushing of nausea to his brain, and he realised anew just what a refuge the Threaded Pit had truly offered him.

And, just like that, with Xeda still in his arms, he emerged out onto the shore, onto the pebbled beach. When he cast a glance to his side he saw the upturned boat, the *Heredimes*, the good old faithful *Heredimes!* He never would've thought he'd be so glad to see it there, in all its ragged glory. Because the *Heredimes* could carry him back to the relative safety of Brinder, and their lodgings there.

And then they could catch a boat away from here, and back to the mainland.

Lou glanced down at Xeda's face. He had passed out about an hour or more ago. He had simply stopped his jabbering completely. When Lou had checked his pulse, to see if he was still clinging to his mortal coil, he had found it frantic, but faint.

Almost *too* faint.

But he was still with him.

Still of this Earth.

Though Lou knew that he wouldn't be all that much longer. Soon he would fade away completely.

Lou watched as Xeda's eyelids twitched slightly, and as his cracked lips moved about a little. And then, slowly, a hair's breadth at a time, he opened his eyes just a crack.

A narrow *hiss* emanated from the pit of Xeda's throat, and Lou knew instinctively that it was because of the sun on him.

Xeda brought his frail hand up to cover his eyes, to put them into shade from the sun, and Lou could only imagine the pain of the spider's poison that surged through his system. The pain must've been intolerable.

Lou glanced about the shore, but could see no sign of Syre or Lunthard. Perhaps they were hidden beneath the boat. Yes, that would be it. That was where he'd left them, in any case.

And so, with that thought on his mind, he slipped and slid his way across the pebble beach, Xeda still in his arms, his withered body seeming much heavier than it had seemed the first time he'd lifted him down there in the chamber.

Lou shifted Xeda's weight into just one of his arms and then, with the other, he picked the boat up and glanced beneath it.

Nothing.

Just pebbles there.

No sign of Syre or Lunthard.

Lou let go of a long-held *groan*, and he pitched over onto his side, somehow keeping Xeda from slipping out of his arms and onto the shore. And the two of them lay there for a while, on top of the pebbles, with the morning sun beaming down on them.

Lou felt those sharp prickles all across his skin, inside of him too, jabbing away at his throat, and his internal organs, and the breaths came even harder than they had while he'd been deep underground within the Threaded Pit.

Xeda breathed hard and fast, and Lou could feel his pulse going even quicker than it had before. He was trying to move his arm, maybe trying to sit himself up. But Lou knew that he was far too weak to do it alone, and so he helped him up. Supported him while he sat. Like a baby propped up with a cushion for the first time.

A deep shaking seemed to grab a hold of Xeda and he screwed up his eyes, appearing to fight it. Lou wished there was something he could do . . . well, he *knew* there was something he could do. He could cast a healing charm, the one he had begun to cast down in the chamber. But Xeda had stopped him. He didn't *want* to be cured.

He wanted to *die*.

But not quite yet, it seemed.

Xeda's juddering eyes slowly made their way all across Lou's face before finally meeting Lou's own. And the two of them exchanged a long, silent stare. For a breathless moment Lou was completely certain that he could see the ice magic within Xeda, down there, peering out from the depths of his eyeballs. And that Xeda's strength had finally returned.

And his first act would be to destroy Lou.

But when Xeda parted his lips and let go of a dry, musty breath, Lou knew that this was a spent being. One which was skirting the murky twilight of life and death.

"Down . . . down in the . . . the"—Xeda blinked hard several times and then gave a rasping breath, the sunlight surely taking its toll on him now—"in the *chamber*."

Lou felt tears welling up in his throat, and his eyeballs beginning to itch. He knew that it was a combination of complete and total physical and mental exhaustion. He needed some time to rest, time to recuperate . . . but, more than anything else, he needed to get away from this *damn* sun.

Xeda, though, made no demands to that end. "The torch —ch light."

"'The torchlight?'" Lou said.

Xeda gave a feeble nod of the head and the very slightest of slight insinuations of a smile. "Yes . . . *curious* about . . . about the torchlight."

Lou thought back to it again. He thought of how he had got down there, in the chamber, and how he'd seen those flames all dancing. He had been surprised, of course he had been, he hadn't expected to find torches down there . . . let alone a person.

"Ma . . . Ma . . . Ma—"

Lou didn't have any need to wait for Xeda to complete the whole word, because he knew just what he was going to say. "Ma'reygar," Lou said, helping out the dying man.

Xeda snatched for breath, his smile tightened his lips, and he nodded a little more.

"But, why?" Lou said.

Xeda blinked slowly, his eyeballs now unable to control their constant twitching and gyrating. It was as if something inside of

Xeda possessed him now. Was this the magic, making some frantic attempt to save Xeda?

Or to kill him?

Lou thought it over to himself, seeing that Xeda was hardly in any condition to continue. He had to work harder to piece this together. Ma'reygar? Auch'ray had told him that Ma'reygar had destroyed the Spider Warrior, and that he had reclaimed the magical artefacts.

But, now, Lou knew that that wasn't the case. That Auch'ray had *lied* to him. He could deal with *that* later. When he got back to the mainland of Shellacnass. Now, though, he needed to understand the whole story.

The way that he had understood it, Ma'reygar had wanted to get his hands on all the magical artefacts . . . well, he *had* all the artefacts and then had had them taken from him. So it stood to reason that he would wish to reclaim them. But if he had known all along just where Xeda was—where the Webbing Cloak apparently was, since he'd clearly visited the Threaded Pit—then why hadn't he taken it? Why had he left Xeda alive at all?

When Lou looked back to Xeda, he noticed that he had somehow summoned the strength to put on a full smile, a smile which revealed all his crooked, mud-brown teeth and his darkened mop of a tongue within. Lou wondered if Xeda could read his mind, just as he swore Auch'ray, and Hildie, could do when they wanted.

"Weak . . . *weak*ness," Xeda said.

Lou thought it through, thought through the torches down there in the chamber at the base of the Threaded Pit. That was just what Auch'ray had said to him, about having to walk with weakness. Was that what Ma'reygar had done in setting those torches aflame? He had ensured that Xeda would have to walk with his weakness, be reminded of the fire magic out there in the world outside, ready to strike him down?

Or had Xeda been simply too weak to so much as leave the cave, to walk in the sunlight at all. Had it just been a trick to goad him forever?

Lou cast a glance back at Xeda, met his eye, and he saw the glint there that confirmed his latter assumption was correct. That Ma'reygar had only wanted to taunt Xeda forever with his failure, to have to put up with fire magic in his home for the rest of his days.

Lou supposed that letting Xeda live had been a tough decision for Ma'reygar, and one which had called his friendship with Auch'ray into question . . . but he had sided with his friend in the end, and kept Auch'ray's apprentice alive.

Barely.

But the Webbing Cloak? Had Lou overlooked that? Was it possible that Ma'reygar had had it all along, and that this— coming out here to the Threaded Pit—had just been some sort of an *exercise* that Auch'ray had set him?

Lou knew that Auch'ray was an unfathomable man and one which betrayed almost nothing unless he felt so inclined. Maybe by sending him here, Auch'ray had simply wished for Lou to find out the truth in his lies.

. . . Or, and this one bit hard at Lou's heart, he wondered if Auch'ray had sent him here, to the Threaded Pit, to see whether Lou would be capable of *killing* Xeda once and for all.

If his new apprentice would eliminate his previous one.

And restore some sort of equilibrium to the world, or however it was that Auch'ray saw it.

Lou looked to Xeda, his throat still welling with questions, wanting to know more and more, and knowing, at the same time, that Xeda's paper-thin skin might crumple in the sunlight at any second, that any moment he might slip away into the murky pit of death forever, finally released from his end-of-days torture.

Xeda's mouth turned tighter at the corners and Lou watched as the glint in his eye shimmied a final time, and, as his breath rose up into his chest, the material of his cloak drawing all the tighter over his skin. And, with his back arched upwards, for the final time, he managed to speak the word, in a hoarse, almost uncontained whisper, "The Webbing Cloak."

15

THE WEBBING CLOAK

LOU WATCHED ON as Xeda died in his arms, feeling powerless to do anything. There was nothing he could do. His energy was gone. He had to save it for another day. And he stared at the withered face of Auch'ray's former apprentice with still a million questions on his lips. But at least he had got *some* answers. At least he knew just a little more than he had before.

He held onto Xeda for a long time, feeling those rigid, pointed, fragile bones dig into his own skin, and feeling the dainty weight of the body. Almost impossible to imagine that this had ever been a human being at all. And yet Lou had seen him breathe, and speak, and *save* his life back there in the Threaded Pit.

Now he was gone.

He turned his mind to the last word he had spoken.

The Webbing Cloak.

Was that his final clue? The last scrap that he would get from this place? Or had he just been confirming Lou's suspicions from before, about Ma'reygar having taken the Cloak a long time before?

Later, it was difficult to say whether Lou looked down of his own accord, if the thought of simply glancing downwards occurred to him out of nowhere or if, and at the back of his mind he was almost certain it was so, he had seen an odd, midnight-blue shimmer pass over Xeda's cloak.

And then he knew.

Or had he known it all along?

Had he really suspected?

Lou gazed down at the cloak which Xeda wore now, taking it in with fresh eyes. It was a haggardly old thing, almost reduced to merely scrap cloth. But then the condition of the Webbing Blade and the Webbing Bow was hardly pristine.

So, couldn't this cloak—the cloak that Xeda wore—be the Webbing Cloak?

Lou felt the air leaking out from his lungs as the sun seeped in through his skull, turning him over in a daze, and making his brain squidge up into a great molten mass. The cloak which Xeda wore carried the final memory of the Threaded Pit, of that dank and moist bloody smell. The smell of the spiders? Of Fyutior?

As he bowed his head over the man lying dead in his lap, he felt his mouth even drier than before and the wash of the waves as they lapped at the shore almost occurring on another planet entirely.

There.

He saw it again.

Another midnight-blue shimmer.

And Lou knew that he had got his hands on just what it was that he had wanted. He finally had the Webbing Cloak in his possession. It was finally *his*. This trip *hadn't* been all for nothing.

It was perhaps hours later, long after Lou dug out a hole in the beach and placed Xeda within it, when he heard chattering voices drifting their way up from the rocks over his shoulder. He turned and looked, the sun glowing hard out of the sky now, sending a heat haze shimmying upwards into the air, and making those figures indistinct from the air.

But he knew that it was Syre and Lunthard. That they were returning to the shore.

As they drew closer, he saw that they were wrapped up in conversation, and that neither of them looked back down on the shore.

At him.

Lou stared down at the pebbles which he'd piled up on top of the place he'd buried Xeda, and he felt his heart dipping down in his chest, as if tapping at his stomach. He felt an icy and uncontrollable sadness welling within him.

He had had to bury Xeda naked, he had worn nothing beneath the Webbing Cloak, and he had looked so . . . so *fragile* once he'd disrobed him. And then he'd placed him down in that hole and he'd seemed so small down there, in the shade, out of the sun.

It was like he had been burying an animal, like he'd had to dig a pit for one of the sheep or a cow that had collapsed in the midday sun. Like it had just been an innocent thing, unable to survive in the bitter world out here, unable to resist the elements.

But, at the same time, and breathing in the Webbing Cloak which he now held in his hands, the rough, ragged material of it brushing against his gnawed-up and mottled skin, he could smell that thick, dank bloody stench almost overwhelming him, and he knew that it certainly hadn't belonged to the spider.

99

It had belonged to Xeda.

A reminder, perhaps, of what he had done.

The many people he'd killed.

The lives he had destroyed.

A fatal lesson for Lou in how allowing his magic to overwhelm him, to take him over from the inside, could inflict such misery.

And now that he had the Webbing Cloak, he would live with that scent every day for the rest of his life.

Maybe he'd been right about Auch'ray having sent him here to teach him something, that he'd had some goal secondary to having Lou obtain the Webbing Cloak. And Lou was almost certain that Auch'ray had wanted to teach him just what the blood of thousands smelled like, and how easy it might be for it to get on his own hands.

But there had been another lesson too, and one which Lou was almost certain—*almost*—that Auch'ray never would've been able to engineer, to plan. And that was the fact that Xeda had saved him. That despite the magic which had corrupted him, left him a shred of a human being, he had still had goodness in him.

He had used what little strength, what little magical energy he retained, and he had saved Lou from those spiders.

And Lou would remember that lesson all the more.

The pebbles stirred against one another. That *scrape* of stone rung out over the beach, echoed back at him from the quiet sea.

When Lou turned his head, he saw Syre, about twenty paces or so away, jogging towards him. Lunthard was on her heels lurking back a little. It took Lou a couple of moments to register that Syre was grinning, that the corners of her mouth were turned up in an irrepressible smile, and that her eyes were twinkling bright in the rays of the sun.

But why shouldn't she be glad to see him?

She must've thought he was dead . . . perhaps believed that he would never return from within the Threaded Pit. But he had done. And he stood here now, waiting for her.

She barrelled hard into his chest, winding him as she struck. And what with the combination of the sun beating down, its heat rising up from the pebble beach, the tingling sensation within him was almost overwhelming.

Somewhere, deeply buried at the back of his mind, he wondered about returning to the cave mouth, taking another step back into the Threaded Pit, to get some respite.

He breathed in deep, taking in that sweet scent of hers, the one that reminded him of home. There was a little sawdust there, from his pa and, he was almost sure of it, a little of his ma's perfume. And a little further back he could almost smell out the ash. The flames that had burned Endmere to the ground and brought him here. To this thankless place in the middle of the ocean. The middle of nowhere.

When she pulled herself away, he saw that her eyes were glittering with tears and he realised she was shaking slightly. For some reason, the first word out of her mouth was, "Water," and she quickly scrabbled for her canister and passed it to him.

He took it off her, squeezed off the lid and poured half its contents directly down his throat, savouring the moisture as it swilled within him, hydrating him once more.

Bringing him back to life.

"Thought you were dead, brother," Lunthard said, as he drew close.

Lou blinked away the bright sunlight and took him in. Funny

how he'd only met him the day before and yet now he was so intensely pleased to see him that it was almost like greeting a long-lost relative. He beamed back at him, and Lunthard gave him a hardy smile in return.

Then Lunthard's eyes sunk down, down to Lou's hands, and to the Webbing Cloak that he clutched between them, and the smile slipped off his lips. He held his gaze there a long while before eventually glancing back up. "You found what you were looking for, eh, brother?"

As if he'd forgotten the Webbing Cloak he held in his hands, as if he *could* forget its slightly chilly feel, let alone its dank and mouldy, *bloody* stench. That smell so foul and so overpowering that he could almost feel his mouth dripping with it, his tongue tasting it over and over.

Lou nodded in reply.

"Aye," Lunthard said, and then looked to add something else, before sealing his lips tight. He glanced off in the direction of the boat, to the *Heredimes*. He jerked his thumb in its direction. "I'll, uh, get the ship sorted out then, eh, brother?"

"Okay," Lou managed this time, before shaking his water canister, realising that he'd already drunk a good three quarters of it now, and looking back at Syre. "Better take care with this," he said. "Don't want to run out."

Syre gave him a slight smirk. "Nah, wouldn't worry about that. We found a spring just over there, over those rocks." She pointed off at the edge of the pebble beach. "When we were wandering, waiting for you. I can go get some more water now if you like."

Lou grinned. "Probably a good idea. Don't want to find ourselves caught short at sea, do we?"

Syre gave him another smile and then, apparently on instinct, she ducked into his chest and gave him another strong, lingering hug. And then she headed off back up the beach, those same pebbles scraping together, making that distinctive grinding sound that reminded Lou of a sword blade being sharpened. Or, he supposed, it could just as easily be the blade of a *dagger*.

Before she headed off, Syre collected up the other few, apparently empty, water canisters, and hauled them all off in her arms, off up the beach. Lou waited till he saw her disappear off over the lip of the rocks before he turned his attention back to Lunthard, who was already putting his back into lifting the boat up, to rolling it back over in preparation for lugging it back into the sea.

"Need some help with that?" Lou said.

Lunthard gave him a squinty-eyed grimace. "That'd be nice, brother."

And so, together, they worked the *Heredimes* free from where it had become embedded in the pebbles and between the two of them, both of them letting out little groans as they went, they got the boat down to the cusp of the lapping waves.

As Lou watched the seawater swill up against the sides of the boat, slipping into those many cracks and crevices, swirling about as it entered then being sucked back out again with the current, he knew that he had a few minutes before Syre returned.

He straightened up, feeling that tingling all over him now, and knowing that he would soon have to bring up the hood of his cloak, else the sunlight would become unbearable. He would perhaps try the Webbing Cloak. Maybe it would offer him protection he hadn't been able to previously enjoy with lesser garments.

"What is it?" Lou said.

"What's that, brother?" Lunthard said, ducking down on the other side of the boat, apparently seeing to some ailment or other with it.

"You . . . when you asked the question, about whether I found what I was looking for. It seemed like you had something else to say."

Lunthard ducked all the way down, slipping completely out of sight on the other side of the boat for a long while. And Lou thought that perhaps he hadn't heard the question. Or that he might be evading it. Either was a distinct possibility.

But then Lunthard rose again from the other side of the boat, his complexion as grey as the pebbles which lined the beach, and his eyes sunken in their sockets. "I'm sure you know, brother, you're a mage after all." He glanced again at the Webbing Cloak, and then wrestled his attention away from it, instead looking off to the horizon.

Lou sniffed a slight laugh. "No, actually, I mean, I could just about use all the help I can get."

Lunthard remained fixated on the horizon for several moments more, and then he turned away from it, and went back to inspecting the *Heredimes*, no doubt taking a full inventory of all its holes . . . making sure he hadn't missed one.

"Go on," Lou said. "Please."

Lunthard bent down and retrieved a sodden rag from within the *Heredimes*, one that was various shades of pink and red, and brown and orange, and just about every other colour combination in between. "You know all about Ma'reygar, brother?"

Lou felt a shudder round his collar, but he didn't allow it to affect the evenness of his tone. "Yes," he said.

"Well," Lunthard said, "I brought him out here a few times, brother, all told maybe a good five or six times, oh he was always a comin' out here, though I never knew as to why. But he paid well, told me who he was. That he was a friend of Auch'ray's."

Lou thought back to those torches in the chamber right down deep in the Threaded Pit, and how Ma'reygar had put them there.

But the Webbing Cloak had been right in his reach. Why hadn't he just taken it?

"That was till the last time, brother," Lunthard continued, "then we were just about gettin' a little friendlier, a little easier, if you see what I mean, brother? And he got to tellin' me that there was someone livin' in the Threaded Pit, and that he was waitin' for him to die. That he was always comin' out to see if he was dead . . ."

Lunthard trailed off, and a light breeze blew in off the sea, making Lou's cloak flap and sending a slight scurry of air over his skin. He should have been glad to see that a fine mist of grey cloud was beginning to come down over the once-bright day, but this news, what Lunthard was telling him now, it made his heart pound and his mouth sour.

Lou knew what it meant now, knew *just* what it meant. But he didn't interrupt Lunthard as he finished off what he had to say. "So I'm reckonin' that now he's dead, brother, that he's gonna be back." He nodded his head in the direction of the stirred-up rocks and the sand scattered all about. "I don't wanna be blunt, but that *is* a man you buried back there, brother?"

Some motion caught the corner of Lou's eye and he glanced to his side, back up the beach, to the rocks which encircled the beach. He saw Syre there, carting the canisters in both arms, kind of like she was carrying chopped-up firewood. And she looked so carefree.

So *innocent*.

And yet Lou knew that very soon he and she—*both* of them—would be thrust into great and terrible troubles.

When Lou spoke to Lunthard again, there was a real frosty edge to his words. "How often does he come by here?"

"Oh," Lunthard said, poking his tongue into his cheek in

thought. "I'd say just about every season cycle since I've been bringin' him out here."

"What time of year?" Lou said.

"Around about Midsummer, brother."

"Midsummer?" Lou said, but he knew it was mere gibbering, that they were now only a couple of days from Midsummer. That, soon enough, Ma'reygar would be among them.

Ma'reygar would be coming to Brinder.

16

A BLIND PANIC

A FAINT SEA BREEZE BLEW against Lou's cheeks, and he felt the moisture, the sprinkling of sweat on his skin, being stripped from him and carried away on the wind. He could smell the salty air, thick in his nostrils, and it was almost so thick that he half-convinced himself that he might be able to take a bite out of it.

As he lay back in the prow of the boat, he listened to the gentle flapping of the raggedy sail against the mast, and the gentle lap of the waves up against the sides. Every couple of moments, the seawater would splash hard against the side and a sprinkling of water would land on Lou's cloak, and soak through it, stroke against his skin.

It reminded him of the Threaded Pit, and its dankness, that steady *drip-drip* sound he had heard in the mouth of the cave, and which he was sure he would hear in his dreams for weeks to come.

Along with that dead, curled-up spider.

And her babies.

All dead too.

Though the weather was fair, and the overcast sky a relief, in many ways the journey back to Brinder Island was worse than the journey out. Whereas before there had been the lack of knowing what lay ahead, and that had been frightening in a way, now Lou knew exactly what to expect back on Brinder Island.

Ma'reygar the Fire Mage.

Who some claimed to be the greatest of them all.

The most powerful mage to roam the Earth.

And he would be waiting there for Lou.

As they sailed on, the afternoon sky dimming slowly, and giving way to twilight as Brinder Island appeared as a blurry purple fuzz on the horizon, Lou tried to take his mind off the coming showdown with Ma'reygar and turned his thoughts to just what Lunthard had said, still trying to put all the pieces together.

He could only suppose now that Ma'reygar and Auch'ray had had some sort of an agreement. That Ma'reygar had kept Xeda alive and promised to Auch'ray that he wouldn't kill him—that he wouldn't *destroy* him. And, in turn, as part of the deal, Auch'ray had promised Ma'reygar the Webbing Cloak on Xeda's death.

The Webbing Cloak was now, in many ways, rightfully Ma'reygar's.

And Lou had no doubts about Ma'reygar wishing to obtain the other three magical artefacts also: the Webbing Blade and the Webbing Bow.

Whatever Ma'reygar had in mind when he got all the artefacts together made Lou shudder. Hadn't there been something that Auch'ray had said about Ma'reygar experimenting with mixing fire and ice magic to produce a new, all-powerful hybrid? . . . Hadn't that been what Auch'ray had told him had caused the curse over Ilsnare?

Lou knew one thing for certain now, and that was that Ma'reygar would be coming for him, looking to get a hold of what he saw as being rightfully his. And the only thing that could possibly stop him was Lou.

Lou the Working Hand.

Or Louson Dorf the Ice Mage.

It would make no difference.

Several hours later, Lou had no heart to count them, the boat drifted back into the dock of Irmlesbrook, and he took in the boats all about him, lit up in the torchlight.

Perhaps it was just his mind playing tricks on him, because he hadn't had a good look at the dock before, but he was almost certain that there were many more boats than there had been when they'd left for the Threaded Pit a day or more earlier.

Which boat was Ma'reygar on?

Lou glanced about the boats, as if Ma'reygar might be lurking in the shadows, ready to leap off that ship and onto theirs, to strike both Lou and his sis down . . . and Lunthard too.

If Ma'reygar did come, Lou resolved that he would bargain for their lives. He would give up the magical artefacts and if Ma'reygar thought it necessary to take Lou's life too, then he could just take it. As long as he would spare the other two.

But, as they drifted closer to their mooring, he noticed no strange figures in the shadows, and no one spoke out to them.

In fact, the harbour was almost *deathly* silent.

The kind of silence that put Lou on edge.

As they got closer, Lou shifted to his feet, and then, catching the nod from Lunthard, he leaped up onto the wooden planks of the dock. He felt the wood give way beneath his hard landing and a slight *squeal* from the rotten material protesting at his weight. He tied up the gnarled, old rope, not even attempting to do any fancy knot like he'd seen other sailors do, and then he looked back to Lunthard.

But Lunthard beat him to speaking.

"Guess you'd like to get off Brinder sharpish, eh, brother?"

Lou nodded firmly.

Lunthard nodded. "Sure thing, I'll take a look round. See what I can do. Might even be a ship sailing out tonight if you're on your luck and all."

That would be perfect for them both. If they could just set sail, Lou felt supremely confident that they would be able to outrun Ma'reygar, that they could escape his clutches. And, for all Lou knew, Ma'reygar might not even have arrived to Brinder.

He might not even *be* here yet.

But it would pay to be cautious.

Lunthard leaped up onto the dock, and Lou helped Syre up beside him, then he watched as Lunthard redid the knot Lou had attempted, made it much firmer, tighter. He met Lou's eye. "You're better off headin' back into town, brother, get some food inside you at the *Peddy Nickle*, I'll meet you there within the hour, let you know just what I've come up with."

Lou felt a thrill pass through his blood. It was just so ghostly, the harbour at night, all those ships floating on the waves, gently knocking into one another, swaying as they went. He turned back to Lunthard. "Couldn't we just stay here?"

Lunthard glanced up the dock, all over the harbour. "You'd be best off at the *Peddy Nickle*, you don't want a guard comin' by and shippin' the two of you off to a gaol for the night. That'd only slow you down, brother." He looked Lou over with a sharp glance.

"Besides, you'd look a whole lot better with a hot meal inside you, brother, you take my word for that."

Lou didn't need to. He felt like a shell, all hollowed out from the inside. He was almost afraid that the slightest breeze might blow him away. This was just paranoia, all it was. He had to calm down. That was what Louson Dorf the Ice Mage would do.

And that was just who he *wanted* to be.

Just as all those boats floating about in the harbour had suggested, the *Peddy Nickle* was brimming with life—*bustling* with life. As Lou padded along the cobblestones, slightly moist underfoot from the evening fog, he could already hear the babble of conversation and the roar of laughter breaking out from within.

He saw the vital, orange glow of the fire, and his gut stirred at the prospect of another of those roast chickens. There was nothing like delving deep into the earth to inspire hunger.

And so he reached down and clasped hold of Syre's hand, guiding her along behind him. He was determined to keep her close by. Especially with a great amount of sailors about town.

He set foot over the threshold of the *Peddy Nickle*, and immediately found himself struck with that damp stench of body odour, all seemingly thrown about with a pinch—or a great big lashing—of salt. It was enough to make his gut turn, and not just the smell itself. But that smell brought back memories of the sea voyage to reach Brinder Island and, Lou knew, at the back of his mind, that soon they would be back on board a boat.

If everything went well, of course.

If Ma'reygar didn't find them.

The floor beneath his feet was soaked with ale, his boots made a *squidge* as he trucked along, and he saw that someone had put straw down on the floor, to help with soaking up the spilled drink. But it didn't seem to do much seeing as there were still puddles of ale all about the place. He guessed that sailors weren't the most careful men when it came to keeping their ale in their flagons, or in their mouths.

Lou could feel the slight chill from having the three magical artefacts on him. He could almost see them in his mind's eye, how they clung to his body, how they made a sort of triangle with their aura, as if protecting him.

Or were they imprisoning him?

He turned that thought loose from his mind, and looked out ahead of him.

Beyond the crammed-in sailors, Lou could just make out the barman, his bushy black hair and yet youthful-looking skin reminding Lou of the last time they'd come in here, before they'd headed out to seek the Threaded Pit, and the Webbing Cloak, which he had stuffed into the waistband of his trousers.

He knew that, secretly, he was afraid to put it on. What it might do to him. And he was also afraid that it might call to Ma'reygar . . . though that was just about as preposterous as it sounded inside Lou's head.

Lou and Syre arrived at the bar with not a little pushing and shoving, elbows to part a gap in the crowd where required. And finally they were there. Lou rested his elbows on the mahogany counter and glared off along the bar, hoping to catch the barman's eye.

The barman was busying himself with pouring what seemed like dozens of cups of ale, and Lou saw the sailors all bearing down on him.

Couldn't their drinks wait till after he and Syre had got their dinner?

Lou steadied himself, told himself that he was getting carried away, allowing himself to get irritable. He had to keep an eye on those signs, any of that *arrogance* that might creep in. That was the lesson Auch'ray had tried to teach him with the story of the legend of the Spider Warrior. And he had seen what happened when a mage gave in to their magic—allowed it to crush them.

It crippled them, just like it had Xeda.

Lou watched on as the barman, one by one, passed the cups of ale to the appropriate client, and then, with a glance about, caught Lou's eye and headed down the bar towards them. The brief smile the barman flashed Lou seemed to diffuse whatever irritation had been slinking through him. "Got back safe and sound, I see?" the barman said.

Lou found himself smiling back. "Yes, it appears that way."

"Getcha some of that chicken?"

Lou nodded to him, and the barman shot off along the bar, ignoring the couple of sailors that had just arrived to the bar and were barking out their drink orders.

Lou forced himself to relax, just a little. To not hold his shoulders so stiffly, and to uncrunch his stomach muscles. This was fine. Everything was going to be fine. They had good people here. They had Lunthard here, a friend. He would look out for them. He would find them a boat off Brinder.

Still, he knew that he'd feel better keeping an eye on their surroundings. It *always* paid to keep an eye on the surroundings.

All mottled skin. Ragged beards. Jubbling bellies.

Lou knew that those were the products of weeks—if not *months*—away at sea. But he saw the other products, too.

Chestnut skin. Rippling biceps. Wide, proud shoulders.

Now more than ever he found he could appreciate just how an environment could shape a man. He thought back to his times as a working hand, about how he'd work out in the fields during the summer months, and that as time went on he'd developed muscles of his own.

Raging, great forearms. Hard pectorals. Iron thighs.

But then, as the winter would come, his body would give in to the inaction, and he would find the fat growing back just where he'd burned it off.

Sometimes he wondered just how he looked now.

These days he hardly had a chance to look in a mirror.

As Lou looked over those countless sailors' heads, he picked out the figure that slipped into the doorway of the *Peddy Nickle*, recognised the quick eyes and the lumbering gut.

Lunthard.

However, just as they caught each other's eye, another sailor, and Lou could hear him quite clearly since he jabbered away at the top of his lungs, shouted out to Lunthard.

"Eh! Eh! Over here, you!"

Lunthard's eyes lingered on Lou's another moment, and then he stole away, headed off into the crowd, losing himself just as quickly as he'd entered the tavern.

Lou felt his heart clench into a knot and his blood pound at his temples. He reached down instinctively for the Webbing Blade at his side, and fingered the handle.

"What? What is it?" Syre said, close by his ear.

Lou didn't reply to her, but he reached down and gripped her wrist hard, feeling her smooth skin against his calloused finger-tips. And her frail, delicate bones against his.

Lou tried to find Lunthard in the crowd again, but he couldn't.

He expected him to pop up at any moment, and to come over to the bar. To let them know just what he'd found out.

If he'd managed to find a ship shipping out in the morning for Shildersmoore.

But he never showed his face.

"Here you go," the barman said, reappearing, with their roast chicken steaming away.

Lou flinched then remembered that they'd ordered, and then he looked back off into the crowd again. Still no sign of Lunthard. He thanked the barman and then reached into his purse to pay him.

The barman took the money with a smile and then, with a glance off along the bar, as if he might be afraid someone was watching him, he dipped his hand into his pocket and produced a scrap of paper.

Lou saw that there were scrawled jottings on it.

The barman said nothing as he passed the paper over to Lou, and then, with a steely glare, he shifted off down the bar to see to the apparently parched sailors.

Lou read the note:

Midnight.

Harver's Moon.

Take care.

Lou read it over again and again, and then glanced off into the crowd. Of course he knew it was from Lunthard—who else could it have been from?—but why wasn't he bothering to come out and wish them goodbye? Could he not see his way to doing that?

Lou was right on the cusp of heading off through the crowd, to going to thank Lunthard for all he'd done, when a group of sailors stepped away from the position they'd been previously standing in, to reveal a shady corner of the tavern.

Lou saw them, quite clearly in the torchlight, he saw Lunthard at the table, a cup of ale clasped tight in his fist, and, sitting opposite him, with his back to Lou and Syre, a cloaked man.

Ma'reygar.

For a fraction of a second Lou caught Lunthard's eye before Lunthard seemed to remember himself and return to looking at Ma'reygar.

Lou thought quickly and, remembering that he still hadn't paid Lunthard, he reached into his cloak and withdrew a purse that he'd separated out earlier on to give to him. He called the barman over and handed it to him.

The barman took Lou's instructions with a nod, and then, still grasping tight to Syre's wrist, Lou shepherded her back out of the *Peddy Nickle* and down to the dock.

A matter of hours later, Lou and Syre were standing at the rail of the *Harver's Moon*, a sturdy and much larger ship than the one they had arrived on, and they were floating out of the harbour and back out onto the high seas.

Gulls called overhead, and that fishy smell that seemed to cling to everything burrowed its way up Lou's nostrils. He hadn't even had a chance to taste that chicken, perhaps that would've gone someway to getting that dank, musky taste of blood out of his mouth.

Lou watched on for as long as he could, till the torchlight back at Irmlesbrook had faded away completely into the night's gloom. And he felt a twinge in his stomach—in his *heart*—as he thought about how things would unfold for Lunthard.

He knew how it would be. That Lunthard had to accept Ma'reygar's money, anything else would be deeply suspicious. That Lunthard would sail Ma'reygar back out to the Threaded Pit in his scully craft. And when Ma'reygar returned. When he realised that Xeda was dead, and the Webbing Cloak nowhere to be found. Then he would turn on Lunthard, because who else could have brought someone out to the Threaded Pit to take the Webbing Cloak?

The only hope, Lou thought dimly, would be for Lunthard to sail Ma'reygar right out there, to the Threaded Pit, and then, while he was inside the cave, to leave him stranded.

But, somehow, Lou knew in his gut that Lunthard wouldn't do that. That he wouldn't have the heart to do something like that. In fact, he knew that if he hadn't returned from the Threaded Pit there would've been no chance that Lunthard would've sailed away without having come to look for him.

Because it would've been the easiest thing in the world for Lunthard, back in the *Peddy Nickle*, to have turned Lou in. But Lunthard hadn't. He had acted heroically.

He had helped them escape.

As Lou watched the last of that torchlight glow slip away into the night sky, he heard Syre give a loud yawn at his elbow, and then she leaned up against him, rested her head against his chest.

Did Syre understand too?

Did she understand what Lunthard had just done for them?

Perhaps someday he would make sure she knew. Make *sure* she understood it completely. Because, despite the short amount of time they'd known one another, Lunthard was a very rare thing in this world:

A true friend.

17

THE ROAMING ENCAMPMENTS

THE SUN WAS RISING as Lou felt the jolt of the wagon jerk him awake. He stretched hard, and yawned, and looked about himself, blinking the sleep out of his eyes.

The wheels were turning, jumping in and out of the rutted road, and he could hear the panting of the two horses pulling them along. And the gentle, slightly muffled *clop-clop* of their hooves as they trucked along the grassy muddy surface.

He could smell the tang of the horse sweat in the air, mixed in with the stench of manure that seemed to constantly stick to their hides. He felt his mouth dry and, for a second, he imagined himself back in the Threaded Pit, as if he had no water remaining. He patted about himself and located a canister of water, tipped off the lid and then drank it down.

That went some way to quenching his thirst, to cleansing that horrible, dry, salty taste that seemed to hang about his tongue, though he was almost convinced that he would never—*truly*—get shot of it.

Lou mind felt flushed all out. He guessed his body was still getting used to the idea of his being back on dry land once again. Right back on *solid* earth. Just about every muscle seemed to ache and his bones felt like they might be ready to crumble up into dust.

He and Syre had done an awful amount of travelling these past months.

But they were almost home now.

When they'd contracted the wagon, and its driver who sat up there above them urging the horses forwards, Lou had asked him if he'd seen a large group of people moving over the land. He had told Lou that he'd seen a group of people just as he'd described. And so he was bringing them out here.

Lou had been careful to let slip something about his magic before they'd boarded the wagon, so as to guard against this man perhaps shipping them off some place before robbing them blind. He knew that he had to careful. The two of them—he and Syre— were ripe for exploitation.

And now, in the dim, rising, pinkish sunlight, he could see the tents, dozens and dozens of them, and he knew that they were approaching their people. That soon they would be back among the villagers from the plains.

Lou felt a tremor pass through him and it took him a moment or two to work out just what it was—what it was trying to tell him. Was he pleased to be getting back? . . . Well, of course he was. Then why did he feel so uptight about it? Why were his muscles all tightened into rigid mounds?

And then it struck him, and he knew just why.

He was afraid that now he would have to face his people and they would see him as their leader. That now *he* had to show them the way.

And the only problem was, what with this magical war brimming up to spilling point, he had little idea of just where they might be able to go.

If even the concept of 'safety' existed any longer in the Kingdom of Shellacnass.

But now he had the three magical artefacts. In theory he held the power now. And he could be the one to protect them. No, he *would* be the one to protect them.

As the wagon trundled on closer, now only a little way off the first of the tents, Lou knew that it wasn't a question of being ready any longer. The time to get ready had passed.

Now he had to stand up and *be* Louson Dorf the Ice Mage.

When the wagon drew to a halt, Lou noticed a couple of heads poking out from the tent flaps, glancing about, blinking the sleep from their eyes. Lou guessed that it wasn't often that someone rode into the camp and, sure enough, he caught sight of one of the members of the encampments, a boy clutching a crossbow.

No, that wasn't right, the person that Lou called a boy was at least the same age as he was, but he had a freshness about him. His lips were uncracked and his skin still unmarked from the sun.

Lou approached him, keeping his arms down at his sides, not making any sudden movements since the boy had his finger lingering over the trigger of his crossbow and Lou knew just what a little scare could do to a person in that position.

"I'd like to speak to Sully or Rut," Lou said.

The boy flared his eyes and Lou noticed the muscles on his forearms tighten. "Who says?"

"Louson Dorf."

Lou watched on as the boy's features crunched up, as his lips appeared to thin, and his clutch on the crossbow seemed to slacken just a little. Then, bowing his head, and finally lowering his crossbow, he said, "This way, please."

Louson hadn't the slightest idea what to expect from Sully and Rut. Sure, he'd left them in charge of the encampments, but he had half-imagined, in the back of his mind, that leading these people—*his* people—out here on the plains might be something of a thankless task.

There were so many dangers out here that could potentially pick them off.

But, as Lou and Syre entered the tent and saw Sully and Rut inside, both of them standing but bent over an unfurled map on the table, he felt slightly assured. The way they cocked their heads up to him, and how they greeted him and Syre with hearty smiles, followed by claps on the back all around, that reassured Lou that they had everything under control.

How wrong he was.

The tent stank of sweat and mould, and Lou knew that was the price of the nomadic lifestyle they were forced to lead for the time being. There was nothing else to be done. They had no home to go to now. And they were condemned to simply keep moving on to the next place.

The next place of relative safety.

The tent was chilly, too, and Lou guessed that it was because the sun had only just risen. He thought that in another hour or so, once exposed to direct sunlight, the whole tent would reek of mould and sweat. Be almost unbearable to stand inside for any length of time.

That sour taste of sweat caught right at the back of his throat, and seemed to cause his tongue to swell. He wondered how much of it was also nervous anticipation of when the sun would rise full again, and Lou would have to endure that prickling feeling of the ice magic doing combat with the sun's rays.

After they'd finished with the congratulations, and Lou had told them just what he and Syre had gone through, how they'd *seen* the fire mage Ma'reygar on Brinder Island . . . though Lou left out the part about how Lunthard was now a condemned man—was he already dead?—Sully and Rut turned to more practical matters, to the map before them.

Lou took in Sully more than Rut, since he'd been the one who'd been more affected by his time in the custody of the Royal Guards. Looking at him now, though, with that sleek black hair, and that wiry frame of his, and seeing that crooked, but sure, smile, Lou knew that he'd started off down the road to recovery. That the Sulliman Lou had known from back when they'd both served as scullers had returned.

And though it was Rut that spoke—once Rut got talking it was often difficult to get him to stop—Lou kept his eyes firmly fixed on Sully's profile, a little surprised at how well he looked, at how he'd managed his recovery despite being on his feet the whole time, constantly moving on.

Looking over Sully, Lou realised that he had been eating just fine. That was another good sign.

Rut jabbed his podgy finger down on the map, and a couple of his chins jiggled. "We're thinking about heading out here: Bunder's Dip. Seems like a good spot for the coming winter, I reckon."

Lou rounded the table, and came to glance over the map. The spot where Rut was pointing was a good month- or two-month-long trek, depending on the weather. If it began to snow before they reached their destination, it would make for a long, hard trudge, and Lou was afraid that some of the younger and older members of their roaming community might suffer. He had to think about those things now.

Those things were *his* responsibility.

"Gives good shelter," Rut continued, "this row of caves would be perfect, fresh water nearby, and it'd also be a great point for us to be in to move out when winter thaws."

Lou glanced up. "Move out where?"

Rut exchanged glances with Sully across the table. "Well, we've been thinking, you know, about the future."

"And?" Lou said, realising that his tone was a touch sharper than he'd intended it.

"We've just been thinking about what's going to be best for everyone, you know, in the long run?"

Lou noticed Syre stir beside him, and speak up herself. "What 'long run?'" she said.

Rut caught her glare, and his doughy cheeks played host to a frail, withered—or *weathered?*—smile. "Shellacnass," he began, "it might be better for everyone if we skip over the border"—he jabbed his finger at the map once again, scrunching up the paper a little—"hop into Rozark, the neighbouring kingdom. Might be better for everyone, all things considered. Look at it this way, we drift a little further south, down here"—he tapped the map again —"and we'd get into the tropics, wouldn't be no seasons there at all, and the—"

Lou decided this was the point where he simply *had* to interrupt. "What you're saying is that we should ditch Shellacnass, that we should *run* from our home?"

Again, Rut exchanged glances with Sully, and Lou knew this was something that they'd been considering between the two of them for some time. And Lou felt a little left out in the cold, all things considered, that he hadn't had the chance to pitch in on any of these conversations.

Lou realised that both Rut and Sully were staring at him, waiting for his response. "Well," Lou started, "it sounds pretty drastic, and I can't say that it would be easy for us, to get all these people—*alive*—down there." He paused, thought to himself, jabbing his tongue into the inside of his cheek. "But if it's the best option, the only way that these people can be safe, then perhaps there's no other choice."

Rut nodded along, and smiled vaguely. "That's right, for the time being, the state of Shellacnass, this is the best for everyone. You must see that."

Lou continued to stare at the map, at that sallow parchment, and at those brown, black and red squiggles all across it. "Still, it doesn't seem right that we have to leave our home behind."

For the first time in the conversation, Sully broke in. His tone was, as always, sparse and to the point. His words dry and sombre. "Would you prefer us to still be skulking about the plains when the magical war hits?"

Lou met Sully's eye, looked deep into those *black* eyes of his. Those eyes that reminded him of Syre's eyes back on the plains, back when she'd seen off all those mages. "I'd prefer us to find a new home within the borders of Shellacnass." He paused again, swallowed hard, and then continued, "But if it's not possible to find anywhere *safe* then I see no other option."

"So," Rut said, "should we give the order to begin heading for Bunder's Dip tomorrow morning?"

Lou thought for a moment, and then, seeing there was no other option, that they would only be doing themselves harm out here, being exposed on the plains, he nodded his head.

With that signal of approval, Rut shifted forwards, snatched up the corners of the map, and then rolled it into a neat tube, which he laid over in the corner of the tent. He gave Lou a hardy grin, a grin like that care-free, blond, cannonball-shaped youngster he had first known in the scullers.

How times had changed.

"Then," Rut said, "all that remains is to celebrate your homecoming."

Lou managed to raise a smile to Sully and Rut, but inside he felt his chest as empty and heartless as ever. And to make matters worse, he could feel the sun's rays beginning to warm the canvas of the tent.

He hadn't explained anything about his powers to either Sully or Rut, which wasn't to say that they didn't know of them, but they didn't truly understand all the intricacies.

Not least did they understand the concept that, for Lou, being out in direct sunlight was, for them, or any other mortal, like walking bare-footed across hot coals.

But did they even need to understand at all?

All they needed to know was that Lou was here, and that he was here to protect them.

That should have been enough.

18

EN ROUTE TO BUNDER'S DIP

THE NEXT MORNING, the people all came out to fold up their tents and to saddle up the horses to get ready to head for Bunder's Dip. Lou watched all of them as they went about the process and thought about how he had hardly considered the amount of people out here in the wilderness there really were.

How many people were counting on him.

He busied himself with his and Syre's things, and the two of them worked through them, spreading out their clothes, folding and refolding them. Lou went off to go and refill their canisters with water from a nearby fresh water stream and when he returned he found Syre there, holding up the Webbing Cloak in her hands.

She tilted her head towards him but didn't make any motion like she might be surprised that he'd caught her, or if she was doing anything that she shouldn't have been doing. Her eyes traced his and she said, "Haven't you tried it on yet?"

That question sent a chill up Lou's spine, because he had been afraid that Syre would ask it pretty much ever since he'd got his hands on the Webbing Cloak. And the truth . . . the truth was that he was *afraid* to put it on. Afraid what effect it might have.

But, above everything else, he was afraid that somehow it might call Ma'reygar to him, that Ma'reygar might somehow have a way of 'sniffing' out the Webbing Cloak when it was being used.

Though he would've liked to have admitted to himself that mostly he was worried about Ma'reygar coming to slaughter all his people, he knew that the real reason was deep-seated, childlike fear. He was afraid that Ma'reygar was going to destroy *him*.

And he was clueless as to how he might stop him doing so.

Lou shrugged off Syre's question and gave her a light smile as he set the canisters full of fresh water down among the rest of their things. "Maybe later," he said.

It was enough to be getting on with the Webbing Blade and the Webbing Bow without having to begin to master yet another magical artefact. Especially without any guidance this time.

At least when he had first taken hold of the Webbing Blade he had had Hildie to guide him, and with the Webbing Bow he'd had Auch'ray by his side.

Now, though, he just had himself.

He kneeled down beside Syre, took the Webbing Cloak as she offered it to him, and then he folded it neatly and laid it down among the rest of his clothes.

As if it was just another simple cloak among his folded tunics.

When Lou turned his head to Syre, looked her in the eye, he saw that blackness lurking there—that *pit*-black tone. He felt his heart well up in his throat and the blood pump hard through his veins. Instinctively, he slid his hand down his side for the Webbing Blade, but paused before his fingertips so much as brushed the handle.

Syre's eyes, if they had been black at all, were back to normal now. But Syre looked alarmed, her eyes wide, her lips slightly parted. "What?" she said. "What is it?"

Lou glanced down at his pile of tunics, and to the Webbing Cloak as it lay between them. "I think it's better if you stay by me. If you don't go too far."

"Why?" she said, her voice little more than a gasp. "You saw it again, didn't you? You saw it."

Lou wouldn't meet her eye for several seconds. If he was honest with himself, about everything else, he knew that what he was most afraid of—above Ma'reygar, the *rest* of it—was the dark magic which sought to prey on Syre.

He knew that just as it had saved their lives back out on the plains, that the same degree of power might well consume her too. And once it had been summoned, like it had been already, it would stir away there, just below the surface, ready to pop out at any moment.

Lou rose to his feet, with the pile of tunics with the Webbing Cloak neatly folded within it, and he laid the pile into a blanket and bundled it up. He would be very sure to keep those clothes close by. He couldn't afford to let any of his magical artefacts out of his sight. Because there was no way of knowing what effect they might have on Syre.

Or the effect they might have on her dark magic.

Something outside of the tent drew Lou's attention. He cocked his head back and listened hard, trying to distinguish the sound from all the other sounds of industrious activity throughout the folding-down campsite.

Horses hooves'. Trudging of boots. A slight *scrape* of metal on metal.

Lou crunched his teeth together tight and he knew that those weren't the sounds of his people, of them getting ready to leave, or of them leaving prematurely.

Those were the sounds of people approaching.

And, out here, on the plains, he knew that approaching people was never good news.

Lou seized Syre's hand in his and yanked her out of their now-empty tent. He had already slipped the Webbing Blade out from its sheath and he was prepared, at a moment's notice, to swing the Webbing Bow round and let fly some arrows at the intruders.

Blood foamed through him. His heart juddered. And his muscles locked up.

He peered over the packing-down of the campsite, and to the approaching people. He could see them now, only about fifty or sixty paces off. And he noticed that everyone else working on packing down the campsite was staring off at the procession.

Soon enough Lou established that none of them wore armour. Neither did they have the wispy-grey uniforms of the Royal Guards. They didn't *look* like Royal Guards—didn't have the *physique* of Royal Guards. No, to Lou, they looked like a fairly ramshackle group, in tattered cloaks and riding horses that looked well beaten by the elements.

If Lou had had to guess their situation, he would've said that it was fairly similar to the one he found himself in with his people. That these people, too, were on the run from their homes.

Lou's next thought, as they got closer still, was the bald heads among them. The brown, hobblesmen's cloaks they wore. All men.

But they weren't hobblesmen at all.

No, and right then Lou found himself glancing over the front

of their ranks, to the first face which took on any perceptible detail
—the first face that slipped out of the hazy daylight.

And he recognised it instantly.

The apprentice monk.

Flucknor.

19

OUT OF RAVENSBARK

OOKING OVER THEM, Lou saw that they were *all* monks. Every last one of them.

At first he felt his mind squidge up out of confusion. He wondered what this meant, why all these monks had come here, *why* they were here. Why, they should've been up in the Sable Mountains, back at Ravensbark, their home. Being here, out on the plains, a shoved-together bunch, they seemed so out of place. So there was no accounting for telling just how *they* felt.

Lou caught the smells of their weariness, of the horse sweat soaking their cloaks, and of the wretched poses they struck as they trudged ever closer to them. Lou could feel the gentle morning breeze blowing up against his cheeks and his heart hammering against his tonsils.

What did this *mean*?

As if looking for an answer to his question, he slipped Syre a sidelong glance, and, realising that she had no idea who these people were, and what they were doing there, Lou quickly explained.

She had already heard all his stories of the monks, of his trip to see Auch'ray on the mountaintop, but she hadn't put the pieces together.

Only then, after he had explained this to Syre, did he think to move off his spot, to uproot the soles of his feet, and go to seek an explanation. He picked out Flucknor again from within the crowd and he shuffled towards him, replacing the Webbing Blade as he went, since he wouldn't need it now.

While the monks weren't exactly *friends* they were a long way from being foes.

Or, at least, that was the uneasy relationship Lou was forced to strike with them considering that he was a mage.

As Lou closed on their wretched front row, still shuffling forwards gradually, he saw Flucknor's gaze snap onto his, and that same spark of recognition flood his features. Flucknor broke out in a smile, and he stomped out the last distance till he stood right before Lou.

Just as Lou was considering how he should greet the apprentice monk, Flucknor burst off the spot and launched himself into Lou's chest, and before Lou knew it the two of them were embracing. He felt the young monk's warmth against him, and smelled that weariness off him too. The young monk's breaths were shallow—*snatched*.

Lou rocked back on his heels and let go of Flucknor. And then he decided to ask the question which lingered thick in the air before their noses. "What're you doing here?"

Flucknor's smile lessened by a degree and it was then that Lou noted the deeply engrained shadows beneath his eyes and, also, the several cuts spread up his neck. And Lou already felt a vague notion of what had happened to the monks beginning to form in his mind.

Before replying, Flucknor gazed back over his shoulder, to the rest of the procession as they continued their advance, drawing closer still. And, right then, Lou picked out the Abbot.

Damon Shriversmyth.

Had he grown slimmer? Had Lou ever really caught a proper glance of his physique, or was it just his memory playing tricks on him? Whatever else had happened, the very fact that the monks had clearly trekked their way all the way down from Ravensbark to be here, down on the plains, and among them —*mortals*—surely meant that they'd all been through the grinder.

Before Flucknor could answer Lou's question, or perhaps holding back the answer, Damon had shuffled his way within earshot, and he managed to raise a smile of his own.

Not quite the jubilatory welcome which Flucknor had given him, but at least he offered his hand for Lou to shake. And Lou did shake it, meeting the monk's eye as he did so.

"You must need rest," Lou said, before Damon said anything himself.

Damon puffed out his cheeks and then pressed his lips together, as if thinking this matter over, as if the answer to the question really required in-depth thought. "So these are your people?" he said.

Lou looked about him, he was sure, with a slightly blank expression. He saw that everyone had stopped tending to their belongings, and that they were bringing supplies: food, water, blankets, to the new arrivals.

Lou thought it somewhat incredible that despite everything his people had been through, and all these things that *they* greatly needed, that they could still recognise people worse off than themselves. And that they were still willing to give.

He couldn't simply allow Ma'reygar to destroy these people.

Thinking about it now, these people *were* the Kingdom of Shellacnass, the very bedrock of the kingdom. Without them—without human kindness—what was the point of it all?

As Lou took in the rest of the monks among them, his eyes sweeping across them all, he caught sight of a pair of faces he recognised too. But, unlike the others, they weren't monks at all. They were familiar faces that he'd seen in what seemed like a previous life.

The face of Old Man Junth and, his son, Herbert Junth.

Lou looked away on the pretence of seeing to Damon.

Inside of the tent, in which Sully and Rut had previously spread out the map of the area, and shown Lou their plans to head for Bunder's Dip, Lou saw to finding food and water for Damon and Flucknor, who lingered at his heels.

As he went about granting the hospitality, he found that he couldn't shake that image of Herbert and Old Man Junth from his mind. The fact that the monks had shown up here, at their encampments, was enough to be getting on with without having to cope with something from his past leaping back up out of the shadows of memory.

But now it had, he wanted to get things straight.

First, though, he had to decipher just what had happened.

He turned to Damon, now seated on a rolled-up sleeping mat and with a cup of boiled-up, herb-infused tea in his hand. The tea which the monks had brought down with them from the Sable

Mountains. Lou could smell those wonderful flavours, those mountain berries and the sweet goodness of the long grass wet with dew. It almost made him pine to be back among the Sable Mountains, even though he had never felt that much at home at Ravensbark.

Damon had seen to that.

Though Lou did understand why.

Since the monks acted as the equilibrium of the magical world, it was imperative that they remain neutral: neither drifting towards fire or ice, or dark or light magic, and allowing a mage in within the walls of their monastery was dangerous enough without encouraging him to stay.

But here the monks were now. Apparently outcast, homeless, and desperate. Just as Lou had been when he'd arrived on their doorstep up in the Sable Mountains.

Lou stared down into his own mug of tea and then took a sip. He got his own taste of all those wonderful flavours, of those herbs. He savoured the warmth of the mug, knitting his fingers about its solid, slightly chipped porcelain.

Outside the tent, Lou could hear the babble of conversation as the monks spoke with the people of the encampments, with *Lou's* people, and he felt a slight warmth within his chest, glad that the tables were now turned and he could offer the monks hospitality where they had once offered it to him. And he was determined that he *wouldn't* turn them out into the cold.

Just as long as they could bear to be around him, that was.

Damon drained his mug and then set it down into the crushed long grass at his feet—long ago they'd packed away the ground sheets in preparation to break camp. With steam still rising from his mug, swilling up in the air, and somehow twirling its way up Lou's nose, Damon began his explanation.

"Ma'reygar," he said.

Just the name sent a shiver up Lou's spine. He waited. Thought it over. And then he rose his head and answered Damon. "What's happened?"

Damon shook his head, his slightly doughy cheeks losing any trace of a smile they'd once possessed and the hardness in his eyes getting a little more stony. "Ravensbark is lost," he said.

Lou felt a tingle pass through him. Though it was what he'd expected—why else would the monks be out here on the plains?—hearing Damon actually put it into words took him back slightly. Ravensbark, with its charcoal-black walls, its fortress-like appearance, well, Lou had somehow thought of it as being impenetrable.

"How?" Lou said.

"Ma'reygar," Damon answered again.

Lou thought hard on it, staring at the crushed grass at his feet, and feeling the last of the warmth leaving the mug of tea he clasped in his fist. He shook his head. "That's impossible," he said, and then looked up to meet Damon's eye. "I mean, I—*we*, me and my sis, we saw him over on Brinder Island. I don't see how he could have travelled so quickly."

Damon gave Lou a wry smile. "Ma'reygar didn't see the need to put in an appearance himself, but those that came, those that came to take down Ravensbark, they were under Ma'reygar's orders."

Lou frowned. "Why would they be under Ma'reygar's orders?"

"Because Ma'reygar is now the High Chair of the Magical Council.

An iciness entered the air around them and Lou thought that it was as if Ma'reygar had stepped into the room himself, that he had imposed himself on their concentration despite not being there. Not able to be *anywhere* near them.

Lou knew that, at the very most, Ma'reygar would be in a boat right at that moment, headed across the sea, on his way back to the mainland. And, sure, perhaps he was angry. Perhaps he had . . . had *killed* Lunthard for leading Lou to the Threaded Pit—to the Webbing Cloak, but Lou was almost certain that Ma'reygar wouldn't be able to reach them before they travelled on.

But Ma'reygar as the High Chair of the Magical Council? It just made no sense. Thinking of what Auch'ray had told him, about how Ma'reygar had once been the High Chair only to be stripped of the role because of his reluctance to give up the magical artefacts, Lou couldn't see how it might be that the Magical Council had changed its mind so radically.

Then again, what did Lou really know of the Magical Council?

He turned his attention back to Damon who was eyeing Lou over the rim of his mug. "You have heard the news that has passed through the land?"

"You mean about Herimyre becoming king?"

Damon nodded. "Do you understand what it means?"

Lou thought this over. He thought about when he'd heard the news, analysed his response to it. He knew that he had been the one to kill the king, and that he would never forget it. The first person he had killed with the Webbing Blade . . .

And so, he seemed almost unable to separate the personal from the political. Like he couldn't quite muster the belief that he had *personally* influenced the whole of the kingdom. That he had brought on consequences. And, from the way that Damon held himself, Lou knew that there *were* consequences.

Damon's eyes lingered on Lou's for a long while, and then he continued. "During his time as Captain of the Royal Guards, Herimyre made it his mission to eliminate magic from the kingdom, though he was glad enough to have it banished to the Sable Mountains—at least kept at an arm's length from what he sees as Ilsnare's sphere of influence."

Damon paused, stared down into his empty mug of tea. "Though, I suppose after the curse Ma'reygar cast over the land, his anger might well seem more justified."

He gazed long and hard at Lou. "And now, the Magical Council, inspired by Ma'reygar, has decided that now is the time for them to take a pre-emptive strike—to *seize* control of Ilsnare, of the throne, and to put to death any intention that Herimyre might have of finally driving magic from the kingdom."

"But why did they raze Ravensbark?" Lou said, just catching Flucknor's eye as he did so.

"Because," Damon said, "they know that once the monks are gone they can truly harness all their magical powers, and use them without any danger of restraint."

"You mean you'd fight back against them?"

Damon shrugged. "The monks' role is to oppose any imbalance in the natural way of magic, and so, yes, it would fall to us to fight back."

Lou thought on that one long and hard, and then he realised what was going on, just why the monks had come out here to the encampments. But, before Lou could speak, it appeared that Damon had already read his mind.

"You can't run, Louson," Damon said, his tone dry now, and his eyes sharp. "Ma'reygar knows that you possess all three of the magical artefacts and, believe me, he will *kill* everyone you hold dear to get his hands on them." He nodded over at the rolled-up map which leaned up against the corner of the tent, its paper all sallow and raggedy. "You think you can run, escape to Rozark." He shook his head. "No, Louson, that won't work. He will track you down. He will track *all* of you down, and kill every last person to get his hands on you, and the magical artefacts."

Again, the air within the tent seemed close to freezing, and Lou felt the numbness ripple through him, and the ice magic prickle through his veins. "Then what do you suggest?" Lou said.

"We must go to Ilsnare. Join with Herimyre. *Fight* alongside him, against Ma'reygar's army."

20
CHANGE OF PLANS

LOU SKULKED ABOUT outside the tent for a long time. He felt the sunlight ripple against his skin, and the prod of the ice magic within his veins combatting it.

A sharp prod of nausea took hold of him now—near enough turned him inside out, caused a kind of swirling feeling within his chest. The power of the sun was so strong, and he could feel it sapping his strength, the same way that having his skin torn open and his blood bled out of him might feel.

But he had to resist. He had to trust in Auch'ray. He had to walk with weakness if he wished to survive.

If he didn't want to end up like Xeda.

All along the campsite, his people had packed everything up, loaded all their possessions—all they had *left*—onto horses and were waiting around to be told where to go.

Waiting for Lou to *tell* them where to go.

The air was filled with the ash of spent campfires and Lou couldn't help but think back to Hildie, and where she might've been then. In truth, whenever he considered fire he thought of her. He could still feel her lips pressed up against his own. And it made his heart throb in his ears just thinking about it.

And yet, he knew that he was best off forgetting her. She had left him now, gone somewhere else entirely. Now it was up to him to go without her. They would lead separate lives from now on.

The flavour of that herb-infused tea still rang long and hard over the surface of his tongue, and he knew that the flavour of it had been so strong that it would take a long while before it left his mouth completely.

Lou only realised that Damon had been standing at his side when he spoke out loud to him. Flucknor was there too, he saw. "It's your choice, of course," Damon said. "But you must realise the reality—that if you don't go to him, then Ma'reygar *will* find you."

Again, Lou looked over his people, all of them looking for direction, for which way they were to go to find refuge. And Lou still had no idea what to tell them.

Off among them, he saw a young boy, no older than seven or eight years old, and he was wearing a tunic several sizes too big for him, his trousers too were all raggedy at the leg and Lou wondered if those clothes had once belonged to the boy's brother.

A brother who had been killed in the fires that Hildie had set.

And Lou was the one who was supposed to make them safe.

To ensure the same thing wouldn't happen again.

Lou felt the monk's hand on his shoulder, and those thick, sturdy fingertips jab hard into his cloak. "Don't you want to get out of the sun?" Damon said. "It can't be making you feel at all well."

Lou sniffed a little and then made a show of tilting his head back and looking right up into the sun, directly staring at it. He observed the purple blotches form on his vision, and found his thoughts drowned out by the ringing which consumed his hearing. But he didn't look away. Didn't *dare* look away.

The sun. His adversary. And his ally too.

When Damon spoke again, his voice was flat and even, none of that teacher-like quality that Lou had previously ascribed to him, how Lou felt like he'd been given a thorough talking-to whenever he got through with a conversation with Damon. "I see that you've learned well from Auch'ray," Damon said.

Lou thought of the old mage, up there on his mountaintop. What was he doing right at that moment? Perhaps he was twirling that white hair of his about his fingers, contemplating some otherworldly matter, or maybe he was staring into the flames, testing himself against the fire, submitting to his weakness.

Or he could be merely prowling about his garden, trimming his lawn and seeing to his flowers, in the midday sun.

Damon shifted off in the direction of the other monks, Flucknor at his heels like a well-trained dog. "Let us know when you reach your decision, and we'll join with you." His eyes lingered on Lou's for a long time, and then he gave him a faint smile, a *distant* smile. "But, Louson, you must realise that there is little good running away can do now."

Lou watched the two of them, Damon and Flucknor: master and apprentice, shuffle off to be among the other monks, all of them still being seen to by various members of Lou's people: served food and drink, and, Lou saw too, being looked over by a medicine woman—the same woman who had aided Syre's recovery, brought her back around when she had practised that *dark* magic out on the plains.

And saved them all.

As Lou stood his ground, wondering just what order he was going to utter to his people, what would be in their best interests, he caught sight of the familiar faces of Old Man Junth and his son, Herbert Junth, once again.

Old Man Junth was all wrapped in blankets and, Lou saw again, as if for the first time, that he was sickly pale—despite the bright sunshine—and set down upon a wicker stretcher. When Lou took in Herbert Junth, looked for those *mean* piggy eyes of his, he simply couldn't find them. Herbert's face seemed softer, which was odd because he was almost certainly thinner. *Gaunt*, even. And Lou realised that, most likely, he had carried his father all the way across the plains.

Lou again toyed with the idea of slipping away, of pretending not to have seen either of them at all, and he might well have slipped away if it hadn't been for Old Man Junth, in a frail —*decrepit*—and yet somehow resilient voice, calling out to him.

He looked them over once again, and then marched over to them, for some reason feeling his hand drifting down his side to the Webbing Blade. Perhaps it was just an old habit, that he couldn't help but be on his guard when he was around Herbert Junth.

"Louson!" Old Man Junth said, all the wrinkles sinking in around his eyes, creating a network of valleys in his grey, sagging skin.

Lou accepted the withered hand he held out towards him and shook the frail bones. As he withdrew, he caught a strong scent of elderberries, and recalled that it was the fragrance which Old Man Junth had *always* had hanging off him.

Those elderberries, Lou remembered now, had grown on Old Man Junth's farm, and one summer, after they'd brought in the yield, Lou recalled Old Man Junth taking him on for a few more days so that he might earn a little more for the coming winter.

Old Man Junth had only chosen three other men beside Lou, so perhaps he had understood the desperation Lou had felt back then, for needing to scrape together every last penny—every last *grung*—that he possibly could.

Lou could still recall those fistfuls of berries he'd throw into his mouth and crunch on as he worked with the other three men, and how sweet they'd been.

And how awful his stomach had felt after he'd indulged in that sweet fruit.

While Old Man Junth took in his face, Lou could hear the gasps as Old Man Junth breathed, as he *snatched* for breaths. And Lou couldn't help thinking that, most likely, Old Man Junth was close to death.

But, for the time being, he tried not to think of that.

All of a sudden, Lou felt like he was a working hand again, and that Old Man Junth—once again—was his boss, and he found his tone becoming somewhat servile. "Are you tired, sir?" he said.

Old Man Junth smiled faintly and then batted his feeble hand. "Oh, I'll be all right, don't you worry." He turned in his place, still on that wicker stretcher, the one that Lou now saw had straps so that it might be placed over the shoulders—over *Herbert's* shoulders—so that he might be carried like a baby. "We caught some luck, at last, when we ran into the monks."

"What happened to you?" Lou said, casting a cautious glance in Herbert's direction, who slunk back from the conversation, his expression looking somewhat sheepish to Lou.

"Well," Old Man Junth said, giving a hard wheeze, "first thing that went wrong was when the skullers didn't show up to work.

Yep, that pretty much did for the farm. Cursed animals ran over the whole place. Had to give it up."

Lou tried to stretch his mind back to Old Man Junth's farm. Standing here with all that he'd done, everywhere he'd *been*, he found it difficult to recall much of the farm. As he often thought of it, it seemed like another life to him almost now.

Old Man Junth's smile slipped off his lips and he averted Lou's gaze. The way that he moved his lips but without speaking, made Lou think that he might be about to start crying, but he did finally find Lou's eyes again. "Lost it all, Louson. Every last scrap of it. We're the only ones that survived—me and Herbert here."

This time Lou couldn't help but look to Herbert, and Herbert met his eye too. There was a new softness there, Lou had to admit, and he could see that whatever trials and tribulations Herbert and his father had gone through out on the plains—perhaps just the fact of them losing their farm—had resulted in Herbert becoming more humble.

And, despite the direness of the situation they found themselves in, and the choice that he himself faced—that he *had* to make today—he couldn't help admitting to himself that it was good that Herbert had been taken down a peg or two.

That he had been humbled.

And now he saw how the rest of the world lived.

What it was *not* to be born into a rich farming family.

Over the Junths' heads, Lou saw that the people were getting restless, that mothers and fathers were glancing about, waiting for an order, while little children skittered in and out, making a nuisance of themselves. The horses flicked their ears and their tails swished at the clouds of flies which descended for the cast-off morsels from breakfast.

Now Lou had to tell them where they were headed. He had to make up his mind.

He took hold of Old Man Junth's hand and squeezed it in his own before wishing him goodbye, and then he went off to look for Sully and Rut.

To tell them that now was the time for them to stand and fight.

21

A FRANK DISCUSSION

"RIDICULOUS!" Rut said. "What's happened to you? Have you got your brain all scrambled?"

Lou breathed in steadily. The sun beat down hard now, approaching its hottest moment of the day. The ice magic prickled through his veins and slowed his heart. The sound of buzzing flies everywhere was becoming unbearable, and Lou was of half a mind to cast some charm to take care of them.

On reflection having something tucked up his sleeve to take care of annoying clouds of flies was probably one of the few charms Auch'ray *hadn't* instructed him on.

Lou reached down for his canister of water, snapped off the lid and tossed it back. The water refreshed him a little, soothed his dried-up mouth. His skin was still slick with sweat, though, he could smell its overwhelming saltiness skittering through the air.

Lou replaced his canister and then glanced over to Sully. "What do you think?"

Sully's features remained shady, just as they always had been, though Lou was certain that since he'd been taken into custody by the Royal Guards his features had grown darker still. Before answering, Sully cast a glance in Rut's direction, then he said, "Hildie here?"

Lou felt his gut wrench. Just the mention of her name. Why couldn't he just forget her? Would she have this effect on him till the day he died?

Lou shook his head. "No, it's just like I told you. The monks said that Ma'reygar is coming—coming for *all* of us. Don't you see? It's no good even if I run off somewhere with the magical artefacts. If he comes across you—across my people—then he'll slaughter every last one to find me, to have someone tell him where I can be found."

Rut, still shaking his head, and swearing quietly beneath his breath, spoke up again. "I thought the whole idea of us heading away from the Sable Mountains—*away* from Ilsnare—was that we'd be escaping this magical war. Letting it die down before calculating our return."

"Conditions change," Lou said.

Rut stared long and hard at him, his eyes boggling, as if out of disbelief. "That's all you've got to say about it?" He shook his head and waved his hand. "I'm sorry, but don't you realise that you're leading these people to be slaughtered? Didn't you say something like that once? Wasn't the whole point of putting you in charge of us so that you'd keep these people safe?"

"You never put me in charge," Lou said. "You all just followed."

"Herimyre will lock us up again if we go back," Rut said. "Don't you understand that? Don't you understand that we *escaped* from him, or is your mind fuzzy from your time in the gaoler's cart with us?"

"If we tell him that we've come to join the army, to fight along-side him then maybe he'll forgive, maybe he'll see reason."

"Yeah," Rut said, flashing his eyes, "and maybe he'll decide to execute us, there and then, in the public square."

Lou shook his head. "No, he won't do that."

"And why *not*?"

"Because I have what Ma'reygar wants, I have something that will bring him to me—bring him to *us*. He'd climb over a whole field of glaciers to reach what I've got. To get his hands on the magical artefacts. We can make a deal."

Rut scowled, shook his head another dozen or so times, and then stomped off towards the bundles of material which contained his possessions.

Lou looked to Sully. "What do you think?"

Sully met Lou's eyes and then his shoulders rose and fell with a profound sigh. "If it's like you say—that he'll come looking for us, with you or without—then I don't see how we can do anything else. Our only hope is to return to Herimyre, beg for his protection."

Lou felt his chest tighten. "I'm not going to be *begging* anyone for anything." And then he dropped his voice so that Rut wouldn't overhear him, though Lou guessed that Rut was caught up in such a rage that he probably had trouble hearing anything other than his blabbering, foul mouth. "If he does betray us again, if he decides to lock us up, then at least we'll be safe for the time being."

Sully smirked. "Yeah, till Ma'reygar breaches the walls of Ilsnare and comes for you."

"Somehow," Lou said, looking off at his people, all of them packed up and ready to go, some of them already mounted on their horses, "somehow I think that we'll be safer with Herimyre on our side." He glanced back to Sully. "Or at least with Herimyre close by."

Lou decided that it fell to him to address the people, and so he did. He outlined his reasons for them returning to Ilsnare, and giving themselves up to Herimyre, and he stressed the point that anyone who wished to leave the group could do, but that they would be risking their lives if they did, that Lou couldn't promise them protection if they did go.

Everyone stayed.

But the looks of fright in their eyes, everyone from the old women to the young children, to the wives, to the husbands. He knew just what the Crystal City meant to them, and that what Lou was proposing was nigh on incomprehensible.

But they would follow anyway.

Lou saddled up behind Syre, letting her take up the front of the saddle. She'd always been much better with horses. He supposed it was because, her being smaller than him, while they'd been out in the wilderness she'd often get the opportunity to ride one, being seen as too weak to march on foot with the rest.

Though Lou knew the truth. That she had unfathomable power within her. Or, at least, power which *he* could not fathom.

As they rode, he listened the *creak* of his boots against the leather straps of the stirrups and he listened to the pull of the horse's breathing, the gentle up-and-down bob of the horse's head, and of the bulging veins in its neck.

That sour stench of horse sweat lingered in the air, and he glanced about him to all his people surrounding him, all trudging their way forwards on their own horses, with all their possessions strapped on beside them.

He so wished he could take them somewhere wonderful.

But there was only Ilsnare.

That was their only option now.

He had decided that that was the crux of his decision. That he had to keep the people safe, and even if Herimyre did choose to imprison them, then at least they would be safe within the gaol walls for the time being. Because he knew that Ilsnare Palace would be the last part of the city to fall when Ma'reygar turned up at the city gates.

In the weeks of trekking across the plains that followed, Lou thought over his decision again and again. At one point he almost gave the order for them to turn around, for them to head for Bunder's Dip, to prepare to cross the border into Rozark.

But he stopped short.

He thought things over again, and again, till it made his head spin.

And then he thought them over some more.

The more he thought of it, the more he underlined his conclusion that they would be safe as long as they were under the influence of Herimyre. But only when he caught sight of the pit-black city walls, of the gleaming glass roofs of the Crystal City on the horizon, did Lou realise that this was his last chance to change his mind.

To turn back.

Syre, as if sensing Lou's inner turmoil, glanced back over her shoulder to him. He simply nodded and she kicked the flanks of the horse harder, leading them to the front of the procession.

Because he was determined that he would be the true leader that his people needed now.

And he would protect them with his life.

22

AT THE GATES OF THE CRYSTAL CITY

L OU'S HEART STUCK in his throat as he led his people forwards, along Capital Road, and up to those enormous pit-black gates. As the sun set over their heads, bringing that pinkish glow to all the rooftops, Lou realised that he had hardly noticed the day.

He had been so wrapped up in his thoughts of how they would proceed when they arrived to Ilsnare—where they were *now*—that the effect of the sun had hardly featured in his mind.

Oh sure, he'd felt his blood frothing away and his heart bucking and bobbing, but those reactions had waned, been relegated to the brink of his mind.

And he wondered if he was now truly learning to walk with weakness.

He eyed up the ramparts, looked to the men who were watching their approach—the men wearing the pale grey uniforms of the Royal Guards, and Lou felt a tingle pass through his blood.

This truly was his last chance now.

When he had fled Ilsnare it had been because he had killed the king.

What might they do to *him* here?

The guards appeared to confer up on the ramparts and then, with a juddering motion, the gates rolled back, opening up that intermediate section which Lou recalled from the first time he had come to Ilsnare.

Again he could smell that dank, musky bloody scent from the Threaded Pit . . . from the Webbing Cloak, and it almost knocked him out of the saddle. That nausea returned too, perhaps the effects of having been out in the sun all day finally catching up with him. More than once he tasted the stinging bile at the back of his throat.

As he led his people in through those pit-black gates, he looked up to the ramparts, to the guards looking down on them, all of them with crossbows clutched in their hands.

All pointed at Lou's heart.

The urge to grab for the Webbing Bow, to slip an arrow into the notch and take aim, was great, but Lou resisted. Because he knew that despite being a mage—and if he wasn't one now, then when would he be?—those guards' crossbow bolts would just as easily stop his heart as they would any mortal.

Once the doors had slammed shut behind them, and cut off all retreat to the plains—but also the entrance of any cursed animals —the guards struck up the direct conversation.

Lou stated his terms. Told them what he required. That he had to speak with Herimyre.

The guards spoke among themselves, their words impossible to hear from way down at ground level, and then, with a slight head rush, Lou watched the inner doors, the doors which led to the Crystal City, ebb backwards to welcome them inside.

If *welcome* was the right word.

All at once, the Royal Guards were upon them, asking questions, mingling among Lou's people. They were searching for the leader, the one they'd spoken with just a few minutes before. And Lou knew that now it was his time.

He dismounted the horse, slipping down off the saddle and landing with a slightly ungraceful *thud*. He looked the Royal Guards over, peered at their faces within those gleaming helmets strapped under their chins, with their crossbows tight in their grasp, held at the base of their ribcages, ready to fire at a second's notice.

"We have to see Herimyre," Lou said.

One of the Royal Guards, a broad man with a firm, square chin, strutted up to him. He widened his eyes as he spoke. "That's *King* Herimyre to you."

"My apologies," Lou said, "I'm tired. We've been travelling for days and days to get here."

"And why's that exactly? You lot don't sound like you're from here. Why've you come?"

"Because I have a proposal for the king."

The Royal Guard smirked a touch, and his crossbow, just for a second, sagged in his grip. "Yeah, and I've got a proposal for the sky gods." His expression steeled once again. "Go on. If it's important enough for the king to hear it then you'd better tell me first."

Lou glanced round him, realised that both Sully and Rut were standing at his shoulder, and that both of them wore tight, anxious expressions. And why wouldn't they? At any moment these Royal Guards might choose to grab all of them and throw them back in the gaol. That would be within their duties.

Lou just had to tell the man, let him know who he was, and trust that he wouldn't be immediately put to death. And so he did.

Though he'd expected *some* reaction, Lou didn't expect the outbreak of flustered activity, of the Royal Guards shouldering their crossbows hurriedly and reaching for the chains they kept hanging from their belts, ready to take them all prisoner.

Lou got five guards all to himself and, before he knew it, he was knocked off his feet, shoved to the ground, and being stripped of his weapons: of the Webbing Blade and the Webbing Bow, though the Webbing Cloak still remained tucked away in Syre's satchel bag.

As Lou lay there, feeling a profound numbness spreading out from his spine to encompass his whole back, like a chilly blanket, he saw Syre being chained by a single guard.

And he saw the blackness lurking in her eyes.

Threatening to consume her whole.

Lou only thought to shout out just in time.

For the first few moments, all Lou could hear was his heart beating, and his chains clanking together. It was like the world about him—the *real* world—had dimmed to a faint pinkish glow. But then it came back. And he found her glance.

And she found his.

The darkness had disappeared from her eyes, and she was blinking hard, as if she was just waking up from a deep sleep.

Now was the time for them to submit. They had to take care what they showed the Royal Guards. They had to keep their secrets tucked away until the final moment.

That was the key.

Lou had hardly expected to be escorted right away to be presented to the king, but he *hadn't* expected to be separated from the rest of the group quite so quickly. There was no room for even a rushed farewell as he watched his people whisked away by the Royal Guards, forced over the cobbled streets of Ilsnare surely in the direction of the palace gaols.

Had he made the right choice?

Or would he have been better throwing caution to the wind, and forgetting what the monks had told him. If they'd have trekked hard they might've been halfway to Bunder's Dip by now. But, as it was, they were in Ilsnare.

He eyed the monks as they passed him by, just as chained as the rest of his people—guilty by association, Lou supposed. And he caught Damon's eye as he passed by. Caught his wry smile before the guard shoved him on his way, and into the stream of the rest of the prisoners.

Then Lou was alone with the guards, and, just as soon, he was being dragged off in the opposite direction to his people, headed through the winding streets of the Crystal City.

As the five guards in charge of him shoved him onwards, *yanked* on his chains, he caught the final glimmer of the sunset. Just as the sun dipped down below the horizon, it set the rooftops of the Crystal City aflame with its rays.

And then, just like that, with a *thump* to his temple from a gnarly fist, the sun disappeared and the flames were extinguished.

23

A GAOL CELL FOR ONE

T HE CELL WAS COLD and quiet and smelled deeply of the grease which slicked up its steel bars. With nowhere to sit in the cell, Lou just slumped up in the corner, pressing his back up against the chilly, slightly moist stone wall.

He glanced off into the gloom, to the bucket of water they'd left there for him. Hours ago—or had he been here for days now? —he had drunk from the bucket, from that green-tinged water. And it had tasted so foul, of mud and faeces, that he had puked it up right away.

Decided that it was better not to drink any more of it.

Now, though, he could feel that unquenchable thirst rising inside of him yet again, threatening to make him mad. Because the slight glow of the moon which swept in through the tiny, barred window above, set a glimmer across the surface of the bucket of water. And, thinking about it now, it reminded Lou of that river back up in the Sable Mountains, the one he had dunked his feet into.

Perhaps when he had tasted the water in the bucket earlier he had simply forgotten himself.

Made up those tastes.

Perhaps.

As he was on his hands and knees, headed back over towards the bucket of foul water, he heard the heavy step of boots approaching along the corridor. He froze where he was, swivelled his neck round and looked out to the bars, to see who it was.

His mind felt like it was alive with a prickling sensation, and a numbness had taken hold of his heart and chest. It was as if being here, *living* here in the darkness, had caused him to descend into himself—to question whether or not he was really alive at all.

But, as the torchlight shed itself over the corridor beyond the bars, and caused him to screw up his eyes, hc knew that he was still very much attached to the mortal realm.

Still alive.

Out of the gloom, Lou managed to pick out three . . . *no*, four shapes. Guards all of them. He was sure. The Royal Guards, he remembered to himself. And they were all wearing those distinctive pale-grey uniforms, their weapons jostling at their sides, stuck fast in their sheaths.

If he could just get his hands on a crossbow or, better, a sword, then . . . *then* he might be able to do something.

But then he recalled just why they'd come here—to Ilsnare. He had chosen for them to side with Herimyre, for them to give themselves up to him. Because they needed his protection from Ma'reygar.

That was the *cut and thrust* of the thing, wasn't it?

Wasn't it?

The glow from the torchlight ebbed back slightly, or perhaps Lou's eyes simply grew accustomed to it. Down here, in this cell, only the faintest streak of sunlight managed to sneak in through the bars, and though Lou had made a point of sitting himself in it, feeling it *lash* his bare skin, he found the weaker torchlight still bothered him.

But he stood firm. Didn't dare retreat. He had to fight for his people.

There was a *jangle* of keys from one of the guards, one of the guards that Lou couldn't see, though he was aware that the others all held back at his heels, ready to leap forwards at a moment's notice.

If Lou gave them any reason to strike.

As the gaol door swung open with a hollow *creak*, Lou stared up at the guard, trying to make out his face—his features. But he got nothing.

His mind felt so cracked and torn from his time alone here.

It seemed so long.

"On yer feet," the guard said, his tone brutish, unfeeling.

Lou could smell his halitosis and the body odour seemed almost ripe in the stale air of his gaol cell. Lou shuffled up, only finding his feet on his third or fourth attempt. The numbness still throbbed through him, robbing him of all but the most simple of his abilities.

He was dimly aware of the movement in the darkness, as the guards swarmed in through the cell doors, and as the cold metal of the chains cuffed his wrists and ankles. Next he felt the hard shove in his lower back and he stumbled forwards, feeling the guards' hold on his chains dragging him onwards.

Was this it, then? Was he going to be executed?

As they led Lou out of the cell, he managed a quick glance back over his shoulder, out to that tiny window of his, to its thick bars.

Could he see the sun rising on the horizon?

Would it be Herimyre's desire to see him hung at dawn?

Would his people be watching?

Lou knew just what he had done. He had killed the king. And for that he deserved punishment. And it appeared that now he was going to get it.

Lou toyed with the idea of asking the guards just where they were headed, but he held back. Though he did try once to put his thoughts into words, he found his throat so dry and so thick with dusty phlegm that he couldn't get the words out. And it wouldn't have done much good anyway, maybe only serving to rile up the guards, for them to treat him more roughly than they already did.

And so, feeling like a ragdoll being jostled forwards by a small army, Lou took in the courtyard as they emerged out from the corridor.

Out here he could see the stars all the more clearly. All of them twinkling down on him. And, yes, off in the distance, far over the walls, he could make out the faint glimmer of the sun coming up.

And then Lou seemed to realise just what they intended for him. They were going to throw him out onto the plains, and watch the cursed animals tear him apart, limb from limb.

Was that what they planned?

Lou felt his ice magic prickle through his veins, that same sensation that he recognised as imminent danger ahead. And he knew that he had to fight as hard as he could now. As hard as these guards would allow him to.

Because if they merely chained him up out on the plains and

left him for dead, there would be very little Lou could do to save himself, to save his people.

But instead of continuing along the cobblestones of the courtyard, of going on to the corridor ahead of them that Lou supposed led out to the city, they took the stairs leading upwards.

Up, further into the palace.

Only now did he realise just where he was. He only recalled faintly after his arrest where they had taken him. One of the guards had knocked him in the temple, and he had forgotten just about everything. But, yes, it made sense that he was here, in Ilsnare Palace.

Where he had killed the king.

He dimly recalled some aspects of the place now, the stone façade of the place, the trellis thick with vines and flowering plants crawling up the walls. He had climbed one of those trellises to reach the king. To kill the man that he had believed to be Herimyre.

Though, only as they reached the top, and one of the guards struck the door hard with his fist, sending a loud, echoing, wood-intoned knock scattering about the corridor, did Lou realise just where he was exactly.

The throne room.

24

A MORTAL KING FOR A MORTAL REALM

ALL AT ONCE the whole place was overwhelming to Lou. The scent of peach seemed to pervade everything and, off in the corner, without turning his head, he could feel a fire burning away. He could hear its coals crackling away. His saliva glands seemed to shrivel at the suggestion and that metallic taste returned to his mouth, the same one he had experienced back in his cell.

The next thing he noticed was the opulence of the room he had just entered, of the crimson velvet which hung from the walls, and of the polished-up, emerald marble floor beneath his feet. And, as the guards jostled him forwards, his head latched back and he found himself gazing upwards, to the roof.

A crystal dome, enormous and revealing the blue-black sky above them, and the dawn stars blinking away for the last time for the night.

And, a little further off, the dissolving moon, and the rising sun.

Lou only brought his head back downwards when the guards jerked him to an abrupt halt. Lou glanced downwards to see that he stood on a carpet, equally crimson as the rest of the trappings which hung about the throne room. And then he realised why the soles of his boots had ceased to make a sound.

Before him, seated in a gilded throne with several crystal beads hanging off it, and with matching crimson, velvet cushions, was the man that he could only identify as being Herimyre.

Dark, cool features, a muscular jaw and bristling biceps.

Though he was seated and Lou was standing, Lou was almost certain that Herimyre would tower over him if he was to get up from the throne.

He took in those glimmering, swift, honey-coloured eyes of his and waited for him to speak, as if the next words out of his mouth might be the order to bring an axe sweeping down on his neck.

To finally extinguish the life from him.

It took Lou off guard when Herimyre's slick, well-moistened lips, cracked a smile. He revealed yellowed teeth with a scattering of black marks . . . where there were teeth at all, because he seemed to missing more than a baker's dozen.

This, Lou was certain, was what a battle-hardened hero looked like.

"Sleep well?" Herimyre said.

Lou couldn't think to speak at all, and only realised that he must when one of the guards jabbed him in his back, forcing him into a kneeling position. And, feeling the air seeping out from his lungs, Lou thought it a minor miracle that he managed to utter, ". . . Yes."

Only now, on his knees, did Lou take notice of that scabbard resting up at the arm of the throne, and the hilt sticking out from it. He remembered a lesson that Auch'ray had given him. He could still recall it clearly . . . though what about Auch'ray's lessons could he possibly have forgotten, or ever forget?

Tysron. Herimyre's sword. That was its name.

And it was one of the most feared *magical* artefacts of them all.

Though Herimyre had no magical blood within him.

Or, at least, he was no mage . . . of that Auch'ray had assured him.

Herimyre, a handful of white hairs glimmering out from his thick black, well-trimmed beard, perched forwards on his throne, those honey eyes of his seeming to match his gilded throne. "Louson Dorf," he said. "You've been with us a while now. A week or more? Enjoying the hospitality of Ilsnare?" He paused for a moment or more. "The *Crystal* City?"

The infused peach smell that rocked through the throne room was becoming almost overwhelming for Lou now. He could feel his stomach twitching uncontrollably with hunger pangs. And the base of his stomach felt like it might sink down, desert him at any second if he didn't pay attention.

What wouldn't he do to taste something as sweet as a peach?

What wouldn't he do to taste something at all?

But he forced himself to look up, to meet Herimyre's eyes all over again, and to put Tysron out of his mind. Because, despite his tiredness, his frayed mind, and his hunger, he had to do the best he could for his people.

Even if it would mean his death.

"I've wanted to meet you for a long time," Herimyre continued. "You really did make a big splash here when you last visited." He tutted, like a school mistress chiding a child. "Not everyone who comes to the Crystal City leaves with the *honour* of having killed a king."

'Honour?'

Lou analysed that word, just what Herimyre meant by it. Had he said it in an underhanded manner, in a mocking tone, or had there been more to it?

Perhaps if Lou had had his wits about him he would've been able to say for certain, but, as it was, he had no hope at all.

Herimyre's smile widened, and Lou noticed his eyes skittering off to his side, to the sheath which housed Tysron.

Lou scrabbled about in his mind, tried to work out just what else Auch'ray had told him about the sword. It would be to Lou's advantage to know much more than Herimyre *thought* he knew. Though his thoughts were somewhat scrambled, Lou did manage to rake up some memories. Little remembrances.

Tysron. It was forged out of *light* magic, and, as with every other magical artefact, brought into existence in the Sable Mountains, acknowledged to be the heartland of magic in the entire world.

The blade had been forged so as to work to repel all types of magic, to lessen their effects. Just as that realisation swept through Lou's mind, he felt a hard throng—a profound *wave*—of heat strike his skin, and he knew it to be from the fireplace, from that coal fire blazing away. And he knew that Tysron was affecting his magical defences, lessening his powers to see off the threat of fire magic.

As long as he bore that in mind, reminded himself that his magical abilities would be a long way from being at the height of their powers then it would keep him in good stead while he faced off with Herimyre.

Herimyre eyed Lou closely. "While it's certainly very kind of you—a *very much* wanted criminal—to turn yourself into us, to the Royal Guards, you must forgive me for thinking that it wasn't a simple act of a conscience getting the better of a man, though you are a mage, and, forgive me again, but I haven't had the ability of granting many mages such an elegant prize as trust." He grinned long and hard again, those abscess teeth like bottomless pits. "I have had some chastening experiences, shall we say?"

Lou knew that this was his chance to get this out, to put the offer on the table, to save his people. He had to act boldly, as any leader might, and try to forget all these guards standing about him, all of them clutching at the handles of their swords, clearly ready—with so much as a nod from their king—to run him through.

Lou said, "I've come here—*we've* come here—to offer our services to you in the brewing war against Ma'reygar."

Herimyre arched an eyebrow. "Have you now? That *is* interesting. You mean, you—yourself—as a mage, are offering to go up against your own kind, to *kill* other mages?"

Lou paused a moment then uttered a dry, "Yes."

Herimyre pressed his fingertips together while he contemplated this. His eyes never left Lou's, and Lou wondered if, really, Herimyre had no magical blood in him.

Because he could've sworn that Herimyre was attempting to read his mind.

"You're an *ice* mage, aren't you?" Herimyre said.

Lou nodded.

Herimyre smirked. "I make it my mission to know my enemy, as I'm sure you'll discover, and I like to think that I can, hmm—how to put it? . . . *smell* magic." He sat even further forwards on his throne, so far forwards that Lou was almost certain that he might be on the brink of sliding right off. "Sniff it out, like an animal."

Lou allowed Herimyre's words to seep into his mind, and for him to absorb them totally. He knew all the stories about Herimyre, about how he'd done his best in his time as Captain of the Royal Guards to snuff out magic throughout the Kingdom of Shellacnass, and now, now that he was king, he had upped those efforts.

Or so Lou had been told.

But now they needed to fight together.

And Lou was certain that he had something that Herimyre *desperately* wanted.

So he fixed Herimyre with a square glance and then came out with it. "I have something that Ma'reygar wants." He paused. "Well, actually, I have several things that Ma'reygar wants."

"Hmm?" Herimyre said, eyelids drooping slightly, and inching back onto his throne, while he gripped the arms tightly.

"I . . . I, well," Lou began, "I have some *things* that will draw him here—to Ilsnare."

"And why would *I* want to draw him to Ilsnare, *mage?*"

Lou felt his chest tighten and the heat coming off the fireplace. Though across the throne room, it seemed to become almost unbearable for several moments. It was as if he was breathing smoke, as if he had ash settling down onto his tongue. The stirring of the coals seemed to fill his hearing with their *crunch* and *snap* and *crackle*.

But Lou remained firmly fixed on Herimyre. "He has destroyed Ravensbark. Those monks, the ones you've imprisoned along with my people, they were fleeing."

Herimyre brought his thumb up to his chin, buried it into his beard. He slouched backwards on his throne and cast a glance over Lou's head, to one of the guards, as if he was looking to confirm this assertion with one of them.

But how would they have known and *not* told their king?

Lou decided that now was the time to press home his advantage. He had to get Herimyre onto the back foot so that he might pound home just how useful he could be to him . . . and how they might be stronger together.

How their *only* hope of beating Ma'reygar was if they stuck together.

If they *worked* together.

"The magical balance of the world is lost," Lou said, "and now Ma'reygar will be searching for the final piece of his puzzle, the last part to truly bring magic to reign over Ilsnare—"

One of the guards behind Lou gave a *guffaw* at this, cutting him off, but Lou saw the quick, steely glare Herimyre shot him, and the laughter stopped immediately.

Once the room was silent apart from the crackle of the coals, Herimyre looked back to Lou, waited for him to continue.

"He wants the magical artefacts," Lou said, "the ones that I have in my possession." He paused again, realising that that wasn't quite correct. "That *you* currently have in your possession. And he will sense just where they are, and he will come here to get them." Lou thought quickly, anticipating Herimyre's next pointed question. "If you don't face him here, in Ilsnare, then the battle shall be somewhere else of his choosing. And we're ready to put our might behind your army, to *help* your army to fight them off."

Herimyre continued to roll his fingers through his beard, to twine and untwine his fingers from the curly hair. There was no way of knowing whether or not Lou was truly getting through to him. But Lou could see no other way of making him understand. Surely Herimyre realised the predicament he found himself in.

Realised that he was on the cusp of revolution.

And the decisions he made now would be for the good, or ill, of the land.

Herimyre glanced over Lou briefly, and then rose up off his throne. He strutted back and forth a couple of times, his boots soundless on the thick, velvet carpet beneath his feet. He stopped a dozen or more times and Lou was certain that he was about to deliver his verdict—his *decision*—only for him to continue his pacing once again.

When Herimyre did think to speak, it wasn't to Lou, but to the guards who stood at Lou's heels. "Take the prisoner back down to his cell," he said.

And as Lou felt the guards take hold of his chains, and drag him from the room, he was certain that all was lost. That Herimyre had just handed the entire kingdom to Ma'reygar. And, in a way, it was freeing. Because Lou was no longer responsible.

The charge had been lifted from his hands.

Though, in another way, he felt desperate, and lost.

When Lou arrived back to his cell he found a plate of pork all laid out for him, steaming away in the growing daylight that dribbled in through the tiny barred window. Potatoes split open to reveal their spongy insides all smothered in butter. Those succulent odours clawed their way up his nostrils, and sent his stomach spiralling away in an unsteady fury.

As he circled his food, his boot steps making an empty *slap* against the cell floor, he saw that his meal was accompanied by a flagon of brandy wine. He thought something awry, and pivoted round to catch a glance at the faces of the guards who had delivered him here, back to his cell.

They remained straight faced, their hands down at their sides. Truly doleful.

Then Lou knew. "This is my last meal, isn't it?" he said.

None of the guards replied to him, but he could tell by that grey tinge to their skin, and the blackened sockets that were their eyes, that he was correct in his assumption.

All was truly lost now.

But at least he would soon be relieved of his mortal coil.

And set free from the burden of his magic.

25

A DAWN EXECUTION

ONCE LOU had finished his meal, and as he chewed on the food it was like chomping his way through ashen logs from a long-discarded fireplace, and the brandy wine tasted no better than the bucket of water he had imbibed . . . or *tried* to imbibe.

But at least it set him free to a degree.

Allowed his mind a little respite.

Only when he heard the key crunching in the mechanism of the gaol cell lock did he really allow himself to truly believe that this was all true—that this was all really happening.

That today would be his last day on Earth.

And as he watched the guards go about the routine of fitting the bone-numbing chains about his wrists, about his ankles, and then leading him forwards out of his cell, he wondered how he had ever allowed himself to see this as a good idea.

He had allowed Damon Shriversmyth to convince him to come here.

And if he had just followed his friends—*listened* to his friends —Sully and Rut, then maybe, just *maybe*, they might've had the possibility of escaping all this.

They might've made it to Bunder's Dip, and never known another thing about Ma'reygar or Shellacnass.

He might've led his people to freedom, and to a new life.

Or he might've just as easily led them to their doom.

None of the guards spoke as they escorted him through the corridors, through Ilsnare Palace and out into the fledgling daylight. As Lou proceeded along between them, he was aware of the *babble* of an unseen crown. And he realised that the news must've spread quickly through Ilsnare, that here was the man who had killed their king.

No, not the man, the *mage*.

And now he would be shown justice on the eve of a magical war, and he would be the first magical blood spilled in the early skirmishes.

And if the gods were well pleased then his wouldn't be the last.

They emerged out from the interior corridor and the stone floor gave way to a rickety wooden platform. Though Lou didn't need to look up to confirm just what he would see there, he did anyway. Yes, sure enough, there it was. The noose. Waiting for him.

As he felt the morning sun brandish his skin, he was aware of the crowd all falling deathly quiet, as if in *awe* of him. Lou heard his heart *tick-ticking* in his eardrums and a knot formed at the pit of his stomach.

He could still taste the pork at the back of his mouth, and he knew that that taste would be the last thing he would feel as he met with death.

Just like with all crowds, he caught that musky stench of body odour, could almost feel it clamping itself over his mouth and nostrils.

Smothering him.

And then, as if Lou had just shifted out from the eye of some storm, the crowd broke out from their silence, and erupted into a cacophony of catcalls. He caught some of the insults, some of the bile being spewed right at him.

Several rotten fruits landed at his feet. Vegetables too. Hunks of mouldy meat. Green, furry scabs clinging to them. Bloody entrails.

Lou wanted to scream out. But he kept it inside. Knew he had to.

As the guards shuffled Lou along, he heard the *creak* and *groan* of the wooden planks beneath his feet and he thought back to Brinder Island, to Irmlesbrook, and the dock there. And then his thoughts turned to Lunthard, who had helped them escape the clutches of Ma'reygar.

Though now that would've been in vain.

As far as Lou knew, Lunthard had died in vain.

For two people he'd barely known.

The worst of it, Lou turned over in his mind as he drew closer still to that hanging noose, and began to take in the details—the frayed strands which hung off the dirty brown rope—was that Ma'reygar would get his hands on all the magical artefacts.

He would have the Webbing Blade, the Webbing Bow and the Webbing Cloak.

They would all fall into his possession.

And all would be lost.

The guards shifted Lou over to a raised mount on the wooden

platform beneath the noose, and they helped him up, still shuf-fling forwards, barely able to move his feet. He waited, heart beating hard against his tonsils, and a numbness reeking through his blood, and looked out upon the crowd gathered there, at the gates of Ilsnare Palace.

The crowd jostled for position now. One person elbowed the other. Each wanted to get further forwards. To get closer to this murderer.

The man who had *murdered* their king.

Despite the chill of the early-morning hour, all of them were red-faced. Their clothing soaked with patches of sweat. And Lou knew they'd been waiting long.

Baying for his blood.

And now they would have it.

Thinking things over now, Lou thought that a quiet death, out on the plains, being chomped up by cursed animals, was a comparative paradise.

No prospect of that now, though.

Now he would have to face the crowd.

With the full taste of pork still filling his mouth, Lou glanced up over the heads of the crowd, somehow managed to see past those faces all struck with tremulous anger. And he looked up to the box which stood up on the ramparts.

To the dignitaries gathered there.

Herimyre sat higher than the others. He held his hands clasped in his lap, and a grey, grim expression fixed on his face. A few flashes of silver shone in his otherwise sleek black hair.

Tysron, his sword, remained in the hands of a man servant, skulking off to his side.

Lou met those steely eyes, saw the glimmer of the sunlight in those honeyed irises, and he knew that he had been a tool—just a *pawn* in this much larger game.

He was the one who had put Herimyre on the throne.

And now he would *die* for it.

Lou stretched his mind back to the nightmare. The one that he had cast off now for a long while. Where he would kill the king. Over and over again. Though it hadn't returned, he knew that the man lingering in the shadows, watching him go about his work had been Herimyre.

Just waiting for his opportunity.

Ready to seize power.

Lou squinted to look deeper into the box where Herimyre sat. He guessed there to be five, or six, including Herimyre, all snuggled up inside. There was another, too, in the shadows. A ... a ... another who ... who—

Before Lou could look more closely, he felt the jerk on his chains. He tilted his head back to see another guard there. This one wasn't dressed in the standard uniform of the Royal Guards.

Not the pale grey colour.

No.

He was dressed all in black.

Just like a skuller.

Lou felt his mind go giddy.

His stomach turn to water.

The sting of bile at the back of his throat.

That pork threatening to re-emerge.

And that pounding, mounting stench of the crowd watching him.

Jabbering on.

Their insults.

And then, before he could get his head around these new sensations, Lou felt the rough rub of the noose slipping down over his head. Find an all-too natural fit about his neck. And, with a *creak* of the rope, it tightened. Bit into him.

Crushed his throat.

Lou scrabbled for air. Breathed desperately. Trying to take down what he could.

He managed to breathe a little.

Just enough.

Enough to stay alive.

The guard dressed in black worked at the rope. He felt his sure hands tighten, then loosen, then tighten again.

This time *impossibly* tight.

Lou felt the blood throb to his head. Felt the blood drown out his thoughts. Scramble his brains.

The guard retreated from him.

Lou was alone.

Out here.

On the platform.

Alone.

The crowd rose to fever pitch. Lowered its volume again.

Lou shut his eyes.

Waited for the platform to give way.

For the hinge to creak open.

But . . . *nothing.*

Not yet . . .

~

Lou supposed he'd blacked out. That was the only explanation. That he had passed out on the platform at the moment the hinged door below his feet had swung open.

And now he was dead.

But . . . *no*, he still felt the tightness of the rope about his neck.

Felt it *strangle* him.

And the gentle mumbling of the crowd.

In expectation.

No, it hadn't happened yet.

Another rush of bile.

He swallowed its bitter taste down again.

The musky body odour of the people pressed together.

Again, he thrust it out of his nostrils.

And the bite of the rough rope, sinking deeper into his skin.

Unrelenting.

Time to open his eyes.

No hiding now.

And so he opened his eyes.

Though sounds were now a dull throb within his skull, and his vision bleary, Lou could just about make out those shapes before him. Make out the box before him. Herimyre. The figure he was *sure* was Herimyre.

On his feet, standing straight backed and proud.

Speaking.

Lou felt the giddiness catch him again. He stumbled. Firm hands grasped him.

Stopped him slipping off the platform.

Stopped the rope tightening about his neck.

Saved his life.

The crowd gave a loud and sustained grumble. They spoke among themselves.

Lou glanced upwards to see Herimyre standing.

Staring right at him.

Lou waited. Waited to see what he would say. Had he said something to Lou?

Perhaps, perhaps not. It was impossible to say.

The firm hands were still upon him. He felt them working on the rope. The rope slackened. It came away from him. And he heard it give a *thud* as it landed at his feet, on top of the wooden platform.

And Lou knew he had been spared.

But for what?

Lou dipped in and out of consciousness as the guards led him back to his cell. His vision constantly dimmed about the edges. Several times he was certain he would pass out. Drop to the ground. Bang his head.

And die.

But they got him back to his gaol cell, prodded him back in.

Turned the key.

Left him alone.

Lou felt the dizziness become unbearable. Felt nausea building up in his chest. Tightening it all the more. And that pork in his mouth now tasted like ash.

His tongue too.

Dry as ash.

He slumped down onto the stone floor. Only slightly aware of the pain which flushed up his spine when he landed. His heart hammered in his throat. His blood pumped through his whole body with greater and greater ferocity. Pumped to his gut.

That smell of grease came back to him. Smothered him. But this time it was pleasant. An almost *neutral* scent. One which cleansed him of what he had just experienced.

Romanced him almost.

As he pressed the back of his head against the stone wall of his cell, he was conscious of the footsteps making their way along the corridor.

That *slap* of sandal he had come to recognise from Ravensbark.

Had all this been Damon's doing?

Had he finally cleared matters up?

Explained just *why* they had returned here?

Because, after all, it *had* been all his idea.

Though Lou couldn't think more than that, because he knew that it had been no one but himself who had stuck the Webbing Blade into the king's chest.

He had done this to himself.

Sure, he could've kept on running, but to what end?

It only would've cost more lives.

The *slap* got louder. Reverberated more about the corridor. Seemed to embed itself in Lou's brain.

He crooked open an eye. Began to feel the nausea wane. And his heart settle.

Maybe death would come after all.

But perhaps this time it would be private.

A *private* death, after all.

The *slap* of sandal got louder still before it ceased completely. And, through the half-lit gloom of his cell, Lou looked to the bars —looked *beyond* the bars.

A cloaked figure.

A hobblesman.

Or someone dressed in monk's robes.

Damon?

"Nice to see you taking my lessons to heart."

Auch'ray.

26

A VISIT FROM A MASTER

"YOU KNOW," Auch'ray said, "you walking with weakness, and all." He sighed long and hard. "Don't get much more extreme than a hanging, eh?"

Through all the mind-scrambling nausea, and the stomach-pounding rush of blood about him, Lou managed to scrabble to his feet. He steadied himself with the bars. Clenched his fists about their cool steel. Slicked his fingers with their coating of grease.

And he met Auch'ray's eye with an uncontrollable flinch. "You . . . you . . . you . . ."

Auch'ray pulled down his hood to show off the rest of his face. His soft white hair hung down to the sides of his face, his slightly rosy cheeks gleamed—even in the dimness of the cell. But, above all else, those star-blue eyes shone out.

Twinkling. Brilliant. Full of life.

Auch'ray gave Lou a thin smile. "I think what you're trying to say is that I arrived just in time." He sighed again, broke off eye contact and then glanced at the bars of the cell. "Can't say I've missed the Crystal City all that much. At least it doesn't look much like they've improved their treatment or understanding of magic by a longshot."

"But . . . but . . ."

Auch'ray held up his hand, palm flat. "Yes, yes, I know you've got a load of questions and that, and I'll answer them all given time. But, for now, I think you'd be best off enjoying your stay of execution, dontcha think?"

Lou's mind buzzed at that. What did Herimyre have planned for him now? He gripped the bars of the cell all the tighter and felt the grease slick his palms all the more.

"Thing is," Auch'ray said, drawing back from the bars and then digging about in his cloak, "I've always kept up a certain civility with Ilsnare, never saw the point of breaking with it completely—unlike the Magical Council. And, as far as things go, me and Herimyre, why, we do just fine between the two of us. Always have done. Been something of a bone of contention between me and Ma'reygar over the years, though, mind. Wouldn't go as far to say we're friends, but we have a certain understanding. A *respect*."

Lou tried to catch up with just what Auch'ray was saying, to piece it all together. From what he could gather, Auch'ray was trying to tell him that he was on good terms with the man who had just tried to execute him.

And, from that, Lou gathered that Auch'ray had used his influence to save him.

Auch'ray ceased digging about inside his cloak and he withdrew a pot of jam. Its lid was sealed tight and Lou could make out the tangerine-coloured contents inside. Already he could feel his mouth watering at the prospect.

His mind twirled back to those memories of blackberries and hazelnuts—what that jam had tasted of back on the trail, headed back from Auch'ray's mountaintop cottage and back to the encampments.

Auch'ray held the jar up to the little light that dribbled into the cell. "Boonurksdale," he said, glancing to Lou, catching his eye for a second. "Didn't tell you that before, did I?"

Lou could only think to shake his head as he locked his gaze onto the jam once again.

"This'll fix you up just fine," Auch'ray said, as he passed the jar of jam through the bars of the cell.

Lou took it from him. Hands shaking, he worked at the lid, twisting at it wildly. It was stuck fast, but after a good couple of twists he got it free, and that distinct scent of hazelnuts and blackberries wafted up out of it.

For a long while he just stared into its tangerine thickness and breathed it in. He was forgetting the stench of the crowd—the stench of their body odour—and he was forgetting the twist of the gnarled rope at his neck.

But, more than anything else, he was forgetting the taste of bile at the back of his throat. And that aftertaste of pork, the last taste he had believe he would experience in this world.

And now here he was, with a jar of . . . of Boonurksdale clasped in his hand. And its contents would restore him totally.

Not having a spoon, and neither having the patience to ask for one, Lou dipped his fingers into the jar and pried out the contents. Watched it glisten on his fingers. Sparkle a little from the weak daylight which passed through the tiny, barred window.

Then he prodded it past his lips.

Onto his tongue.

And he lolled it about his mouth.

For the longest moment, Lou was certain that the soles of his boots had left the stone floor. That he was levitating. Lifted up above the world.

The sweetness rippled through him, warming his blood. He felt the ice magic prickle through his veins too. And his heart leap back into life.

All his senses returned to him.

No . . . they got sharper.

His vision cleared.

His mind too.

His ears pricked at the slightest twitch of the smallest mouse's tail.

And his mouth was filled with the taste of blackberries and hazelnuts, and he knew that he was somewhere close to approaching heaven.

As he felt his thoughts slot back into order, he looked to Auch'ray, all those questions that he had alluded to tracing his lips. Now was the time. Now Auch'ray *had* to give him those answers he'd promised.

He turned to him, keeping the jar of jam clasped in his fist, and he traced those star-blue eyes, staring back at him from between the bars of his cell.

"You know so much already," Auch'ray said. "About the Spider Warrior, what became of him, all of that. And," he paused for a great while before adding, "I hear that you now have the Webbing Cloak in your possession."

"I do," Lou said, feeling his voice firm and sure for the first time in days.

Or had it been weeks?

Auch'ray nodded, gave a slight smile, and then said, "And so you know the truth?"

"Yes."

"You must understand, Louson, that it was part of your development. There are some things . . . some things that are just better off experienced alone. Better not to be filtered through some conduit, not having the truth twisted—*moulded*—into a convenient shape for the speaker. And . . . and . . ."

Lou noted the glistening tears in Auch'ray's eyes, and he realised that his master still felt terrible about how he had misled him. And while a part of Lou was pleased—*pleased* that the tables had turned, that Auch'ray had got his comeuppance for lying—another part of him felt deeply sad for what he had to say now.

"Xeda is dead," Lou said.

Auch'ray first took the news with a slight widening of his eyes. And then his dry lips parted, as if to say something. But, as both of them well knew, there was really nothing to say. What could anyone say?

Finally, Auch'ray spoke. "You buried him?"

Lou nodded.

Auch'ray smiled weakly. "Good, that's good." He paused. "I'm glad. Glad that he had . . . he had *someone* to be there for him. To be with him at the, uh, end."

A pregnant pause grew between them, and as it lengthened, second by second, Lou felt less and less inclined to be the one to break it. But, as he polished off more than half of his jar of Boonurksdale, he decided that he did have to be the one to do it.

"Is it true?" Lou said. "That you made a deal with Ma'reygar, that he was to inherit the Webbing Cloak when Xeda died?"

Auch'ray's gaze grew distant.

A sunbeam broke from the window— the sun coming out from behind a cloud—and it lay across Auch'ray's arm. Auch'ray shuddered slightly, a large reaction considering Auch'ray's self-attested exercises of 'walking with weakness' that he lived up on his mountaintop.

Slowly, Auch'ray nodded, and then added, "Yes, and I was to give him the Webbing Bow too, when the time came."

Lou felt warmth stirring in his gut, a renewed anger ripping through him, and growing harder and harder to control.

Why couldn't Auch'ray have just been honest with him?

Would it have hurt him so much?

Lou shook his head, and stared out at those sunbeams streaking in through the tiny, barred window above them.

Again, they descended into silence until Auch'ray took it upon himself to speak again. "No one is more affected by all that has happened, Louson. You must understand that. And, yes, I have made some terrible choices, but you must understand that weight that lies on a master's heart to see his apprentice struck down . . . or to have the prospect of him being struck down weighing on him.

"It is like losing a part of yourself, trust me on that one, Louson.

"I came here, to Ilsnare, because I heard of the destruction of Ravensbark, and had heard stories of the monks fleeing. When I arrived to the city, visited the palace gaols"—he threw up his hands—"came *here*, I met with Damon who told me of Herimyre's plans.

"And that was why I went to the royal box today, why I called off your execution, why I saw fit to convince Herimyre that you really had come back to Ilsnare to help him with the brewing magical war. And that you weren't simply here to hide away." He paused. "That is the truth, is it not, Louson?"

Lou thought it over. Sure, he'd brought his people here to keep them safe, that had been his main motive, or at least that was what he told himself. But, on the other hand, he couldn't honestly say that he had had any intention of running into Ma'reygar while out there in the wilderness.

Now, though, he had to make his choice, everything else rested upon it.

He tilted his head up and met Auch'ray's eye. "I've come here to fight."

They stayed in silence again for a long while, the two of them down in the palace gaol, and Lou wanted to ask what would happen in his immediate future, just what was going to become of him now.

Would the guards now allow him out of the cell?

To do what he had tried to promise Herimyre?

Or was a 'stay of execution' the very best that Auch'ray could do for him?

Finally, Auch'ray did break the silence. "I never told you about the names of the magical artefacts, and how they came about. Why the Spider Warrior? Why the Webbing Bow, or the Webbing Blade, or the Webbing Cloak, for that matter?"

Lou leaned in closer to him. He could feel his heart beating strong and his breaths came easily. It was like the jam—the Boonurksdale—had thickened his blood. Made him a thousand times stronger.

"Where?" Lou said, looking down at his booted feet, at the

roughly tied laces, and then to that bucket of foul water which stood opposite him.

Auch'ray took a long breath inwards and then continued, "When I told Xeda of the locations of the three magical artefacts, and he swept off to go and look for them, he never thought to come back to me, to seek out my advice once he had possession of them.

"For him, it was enough that he had them. Now he wielded the greatest power of all the ice mages . . of all the *mages* in the world. And that was true, or was true at the time.

"He needed practice, though, and so he stole off to Brinder Island"—Lou felt a kick through his chest, a chilling of his blood at just the mention of the name, and his mind's eye was filled with Lunthard's beaming face—"and it was there that he sought out the Threaded Pit, as it is known, and the spider which dwelled within."

Lou glanced up, thought about the spider he had killed, and how Xeda had wept over it. What had been its name?

. . . Fyutior, wasn't it?

"I only learned that after, though," Auch'ray continued, "after Xeda had returned, as the Spider Warrior, as he dubbed himself, to wreak havoc over all the mortal lands. And with the magical artefacts, those items passed down through the years from one mage to the next, that he had decided to dub the Webbing Blade, the Webbing Bow and the Webbing Cloak."

"So he named them himself?"

Auch'ray nodded, and then gave a slightly wry smile. "Don't you remember what I told you about checking yourself against arrogance, about not letting it in. Because that is the only opportunity that the magic will need to consume you whole." He smiled a little wider. "I believe that you have started off well—you have guarded yourself well so far. You have walked with weakness."

Lou felt a light glow pass through him. Despite all that had occurred today, what with the attempted hanging, and how he had been given a reprieve, he guessed that he still wasn't immune to his master's praise.

And then Lou glanced up at Auch'ray again. "I have one more question," he said.

"Oh?"

"It's about Hildie."

"And?"

Lou flexed his fingers, feeling them stiff and unwieldy. He guessed that while he had been on the platform, with that noose about his neck, that he had unknowingly held his fingers rigid, readied himself for the killing move.

But it hadn't come.

Though the aftershock remained.

"She told me," Lou began, "what she told me was that her father—Ma'reygar—that he inherited the Webbing Blade from her mother."

Auch'ray tilted his head to one side. "That does not surprise me."

"What doesn't?"

"That Ma'reygar would lie to his own daughter."

Lou thought hard about it, about just what Hildie had told him, and he wondered.

He wondered just whose side she was on, whose side she had always been on. And it turned his stomach to think of it, because he couldn't help thinking back to that kiss they'd shared on that bridge, on the path to the Sable Mountains.

That sizzle of warmth from her lips onto his. And that light spark that had passed between their skin.

Or had he just imagined it all?

Lou turned back to Auch'ray. "And now? What happens now?"

"Now," Auch'ray repeated, "now we must plan for the strike, for when Ma'reygar brings his magical army to bear on the fortifications of Ilsnare." He smiled again. "Though I do not believe that it will be too long in coming."

27

THE LONG, HARD CRY OF BATTLE

LATER ON IN THE DAY, Lou was met with the same guards from before.

Like before, they carried a large loop of keys, but, unlike before, they did not have the clanking chains along with them.

They worked quickly to let Lou free from his cell.

As Lou followed them out, he cast a final glance at that bucket of foul water, of that water that he had resorted to drinking when he had come to the very lowest of his desperate thirst. And he resolved, as far as it would be possible, not to become imprisoned again.

Luckily, he supposed, with this coming magical war, that wasn't too large of a possibility.

Most likely, he would end up dead.

~

Still with that foul water on his mind, Lou followed the guards round the curving corridors and over the sturdy stone floors. He listened to their footsteps echo around and he couldn't help feeling a slight brightness in his mood since he supposed that he was well on the way to going free.

Lou followed the guards up several flights of spiral steps, and felt his mind going round in circles, and that nausea that had struck him down before threatening to make another appearance.

But he warded it off.

Chewed hard on his lip, and battled on.

The guards brought him up into a small stone room about three quarters up one of the turrets which stood up on the ramparts of Ilsnare Palace. Once inside, all but one of the guards left him. And, of course, the guard continued to carry a dagger at his belt, and a crossbow slung over his shoulder.

Ready for any resistance.

Lou took in the room about him.

A compact, low-lying bed with a rough-looking blanket folded on top. And a mahogany trunk—large enough to serve as a coffin —laid at the foot of the bed. There was a window which looked out over the plains which encircled Ilsnare, and Lou could make out that thatch of trees, the forest where he and his people had escaped through when they'd fled Ilsnare.

And now they were back.

He took the remaining guard's silence as an invitation for him to step into the room, and so he did, going immediately over to the bed and then sitting.

The springs creaked hard beneath his weight.

The mattress was squashy, well worn, but it was a welcome relief from that stone floor down in his gaol cell.

As he breathed in the air of the tiny room, he caught dust up his nose, along with that endless scent of the stone all around him. Getting the dust caught up his nose reminded him of when he would go into his pa's workshop and breathe in the sawdust lying about.

The sawdust had affected him just as much as the dust affected him now.

He held up the sleeve of his tunic to mute his sneeze, and succeeded. Once he'd suppressed it, he looked up to meet the guard's eye. "Where's all my stuff?" Lou said.

The guard held Lou's gaze for just another moment, and then looked to the trunk at the foot of the bed.

Lou rocked onto his feet and went over to it. Unclasped it, and swung the lid back to look at what was inside.

In there he found his spare tunics, trousers, his belt, among other things.

But there were some notable exceptions.

He turned back to the guard again. "Where're my weapons?"

The guard said nothing.

Lou looked back to the trunk once again.

Yes, everything was here, all nestled inside. When Lou breathed in the interior he caught a whiff of the mahogany.

He guessed that, for now, he would have to be content with his freedom.

He could pick the bones about his weapons later on.

As he pawed through his clothes, looking forwards to shucking the clothes he'd been wearing while he'd been down in his gaol cell, he noticed something that he was sure—if whoever had pried through his belongings had been paying attention—shouldn't have been there.

The Webbing Cloak.

Lou's chest prickled, and he felt the magic within his veins rush about, as if excited. A strange, almost otherworldly *hum* struck a chord inside his mind.

Lou had to work hard to conceal his delight at finding it there, and so, before he turned back round, he made sure to wipe the smile off his face. He glanced off at the guard. "So you're here to look after me, are you?"

Again, the guard said nothing at all.

"Could you at least show me the way to the toilet? And I'd like to have a wash if at all possible."

The guard held his neutral stare for another few seconds and then took a step back, into the corridor, and then trod onwards, apparently waiting for Lou to follow.

Once Lou got himself all soaped up, all sponged down, and dressed in clean—and *nice*-smelling—clothes, he sat on the edge of his bed and watched the sun sinking down on the horizon.

He watched the rooftops of the Crystal City catch alight, and glimmer with the final sunrays. That pinkish glow, it was almost dreamlike to Lou. And, he supposed, in a way it was. Back when he had been a working hand he never—*ever*—would've dreamed that he'd ever get to visit the Crystal City.

And yet, look where he was now.

. . . And then some.

Lou heard yet more boot steps out in the corridor, someone else padding their way up the stone steps. And so he waited patiently, watching for the figure who would emerge.

A well-kept, youngish boy appeared, wearing—what Lou supposed to be—the dress of the king's court. At least the tunic the boy wore was woven with silver and gold thread, and what looked like rubies hung off the tunic from thin, bronze strands.

Lou looked to his guard, as if he might have to give this boy permission to enter. But, as it was, the guard didn't seem the least bit interested, choosing instead to stare over Lou's head, out onto the plains which surrounded Ilsnare.

Or, perhaps, like Lou, he was observing those rooftops.

Maybe, despite having surely grown up here, in Ilsnare, the guard still hadn't got over that sight.

Lou knew that he would never get over the sight himself.

The boy instructed Lou to follow him down the stairs, and deeper into the palace. And as they went along, Lou noticed that his guard was following a little way behind. But, he supposed, trust was something that had to be earned, rather than thrown about.

That was what made it valuable.

At least he *only* had one guard this time.

Rather than the four or five he'd had before.

And no chains.

Lou had imagined that they'd be headed for the throne room, for some sort of frank discussion with Herimyre, and so he was fairly pleased to notice they were on their way to the banquet room—a fact he divined from the scent of roasting shanks of meat carrying on the air, all sprinkled with herbs.

He could almost hear the crackle of the fat in the flames too.

The banquet hall was already stuffed full. The guards, all still wearing their pale grey uniforms, and all of them still wearing their weapons, tucked into their dinner.

Most gripped tight to their shanks of meat and ripped it from its bone with their teeth.

Lou could hardly contain his hunger. He could feel it itching about inside of his stomach, threatening to burst out of him if he didn't do something about it soon.

He identified Auch'ray, seated across the hall, with the king.

With Herimyre.

Lou felt a shiver pass up his spine. And he knew it wasn't from the fireplace crackling away. It was because the last time he had seen the king—the last time he had seen Herimyre—it had been while he'd been standing out on that wooden platform, ready to be hung by the neck till dead.

And so this situation seemed a mite surreal.

But there was nothing to be done.

He had to act natural.

Or as natural as he could manage.

He skirted along the long wooden benches. Felt those guards' eyes lolling over him. Everyone recognised him. Of course they did. The royal *murderer*. Given a reprieve.

He met Auch'ray's eye almost immediately, as if asking permission from him, rather than the king, to sit.

Auch'ray gave him a stern nod and Lou sat.

"Is your room to your satisfaction?" Herimyre said, taking another shank of meat from the pile before him.

Lou eyed the slick grease dribbling down the pile of meat. And the speckle of herbs on each. The flame-burned meat. He wondered how long it had really been since he'd eaten a full and proper meal.

"Oh, yes," Lou said, answering Herimyre's question about his room, "just fine."

Herimyre slipped Lou the shred of a smile and then tucked into his freshly taken shank of meat. He ripped it off the bone with his teeth. Just like the men.

One thing that Lou noticed, looking around the hall, was that none of the guards had any flagons of wine before them. Nothing. Just water.

Stranger still, when Lou looked off to his side, to the king, he saw that he too only drank water.

He supposed he had imagined something quite different.

But, then again, he guessed that the king—the *new* king—had been a soldier himself.

And, with a battle soon to be fought, maybe he realised this was not the time for celebration.

"Quite a show today, hmm?" Herimyre said, in between mouthfuls of meat.

Lou felt his chest tighten. His mouth went dry. He reached for the jug of water which sat on the table before them, grasped a hold of the handle. And then his grip slipped.

The wooden water jug toppled over.

Water splashed all over the table.

All over Herimyre—the *king's*—lap.

Herimyre, however, remained seated. Unmoved by the slip.

"I . . . I'm sorry," Lou said.

Without making eye contact or reacting in any way to the water lying on his lap, Herimyre continued to tuck into his meat. He even slipped Lou a sidelong wry smile. "Quite all right," he said. "I imagine your nerves are somewhat wrangled after the day you've had."

"Yes," Lou replied, feeling for the first time that the jam might be wearing off—and that the weariness from spending so long down there in the gaol was beginning to kick in.

Herimyre ripped off another chunk of meat with his teeth and chewed it up, apparently completely indifferent to anything else around him.

Totally immersed by the shank of meat he clutched in his fist.

Before Lou had to think of some conversation-starter, a servant arrived to lay a plate at Lou's place. Lou thanked him and then, seeing the rest of the table were all chewing away—like Herimyre —on their shanks of meat, he served himself.

And it was a quiet, if slightly tense, dinner.

But, Lou had to admit, he felt fully regenerated following it.

Once all the dirty plates had been cleared by the servants, and Herimyre had flapped away servants who wanted to dry him, or the table around him from where Lou had overturned the jug of water, Lou looked to Herimyre to see him dabbing his lips with a napkin. He caught Lou's eye too. And before Lou could think to look away—out of politeness, or so he told himself—Herimyre spoke to him.

"Two factors," he said, "have saved you from the gallows today."

Lou flinched. Couldn't manage to contain himself. He gripped the wooden bench below him tight with his fingers. He knew that at any moment Herimyre might bite him. Like a rabid dog . . . like one of those *cursed* animals which plagued Ilsnare's evenings and early mornings.

"The first," Herimyre continued, "was your master, an acquaintance of mine, and one whose opinion I hold in high regard, since, from time to time, he has advised me expertly on certain matters. And so, when he came to me, on the day of your execution, and informed me that it would be truly the *wrong* thing to do, I gave him my full attention."

He gave a wry smile. "I suppose that says quite a lot about the regard which I hold Auch'ray, does it not?"

Lou found himself gibbering out an agreement. He briefly caught Auch'ray's eye across the table. And didn't receive the assured glance he might've expected.

No, Auch'ray appeared apprehensive. His eyes never settled. Those quick, smart, *swift* star-blue eyes were constantly on the move.

Lou turned his attention back to Herimyre.

"Yes," Herimyre continued, "Auch'ray told me that it was for the greater good to keep you alive, not to allow you to be killed." He paused for a long moment. "For me to overlook your, ah, *infraction* in the past." This time Herimyre gave a bold-faced grin. "Though, I must admit, the king's demise has been something to my benefit." The smile slipped off his lips. "Though I do realise that *I* must have been the intended target—the one you sought out."

Lou felt a chill pass through him. His ice magic pricked his veins and stirred his heart. But he knew everything Herimyre said was true.

He could contest nothing at all.

And so he stayed quiet.

"Yes, it is with no doubt that without Auch'ray's advice, this second factor would not have saved you. But I can see now, with no little help from Auch'ray, that it may well have been the wisest thing to keep you alive."

"And what's the second factor?" Lou said, as surprised as anyone that he managed to get the words out, since he had begun to tremble profoundly.

Herimyre turned his head round so that he eyeballed Lou, held him completely and totally transfixed by his stare. "The second factor," Herimyre said, "is that my scouts, this very morning, arrived back from the plains, and they report that Ma'reygar's army has now advanced into a position which suggests they wish to launch their attack tomorrow. Early, is the thinking, *first thing*."

This time it was Herimyre who broke off the stare, and turned his attention to his flagon of water. He stared into it long and hard as if it were some vicious animal. "While I have lived my life, always believed that I have the strength to repel magic, with the aid of my sword—with Tysron—it now appears to me that I can use all the friends I can get, whether mortal or mage."

He snapped his head back upright, again his eyes tracing Lou's. "And so, it now falls to me to ask Auch'ray, the monks, and you—Louson—whether you shall join forces and fight shoulder to shoulder as we try to see this strike off. Try to bring some peace back to the kingdom."

Lou didn't look away, nor did he flinch at all. He stared back into those honey-soaked eyes of Herimyre's and gave him a doleful, and stern, nod.

28

WORDS OF WISDOM

THERE WAS LITTLE TIME to waste with preparations for the forthcoming battle, and Lou soon returned to his room, to the tiny room, with Auch'ray alongside him. Though he had fought his case with Herimyre, he had failed to convince him to give him his weapons now:

For him to hand back the Webbing Blade and the Webbing Bow to Lou in preparation for the battle.

And Lou supposed that Herimyre had somewhat overestimated him. Thought too much of him. Thought that, if Lou willed it, he could go on a rampage through Ilsnare Palace, tear the place down with his hands on the magical artefacts.

If only he'd known the truth.

That Lou, very much, at least to his mind, was an apprentice.

But at least he had his master nearby.

Auch'ray trod over the stone slabs, his sandals making that distinctive *slap* as he went along, and he opened up the chest without a word to Lou. After a moment of digging round inside, he came up with the Webbing Cloak, which he held up, pinned to his chest, as if he were seeing if it might fit him.

Lou was certain that Auch'ray would be able to wield far more power than he could if he wore the Webbing Cloak.

Why did Lou have to be the responsible one?

His powers were nothing when compared to Ma'reygar.

"Have you tried it on yet?" Auch'ray said, those star-blue eyes twinkling in the moonlight which dripped in through the window of the room.

Lou shook his head.

"Maybe now's the time."

"What'll it do?"

Auch'ray fixed Lou hard with his glare, and then turned his attention downwards, his focus drifting once more back to the Webbing Cloak itself. "The Webbing Cloak is much more subtle than the other artefacts. Whereas the Webbing Blade *cuts*, and the Webbing Bow lets fly *arrows*, the Webbing Cloak acts more passively. It does not inflict itself on the enemy, but it doesn't help him either. It allows the user to better slip into the wind, to disappear into the shadows, to focus and channel magical energy of brutal proportions."

"And you think it'll be the difference between me beating or being defeated by Ma'reygar?"

"Oh, undoubtedly, Louson. Undoubtedly."

"And," Lou said, already feeling his throat stick, and the churn of his stomach still dealing with the rich dinner he'd just ingested, "do you believe that I can beat him?"

Auch'ray took some time to consider this, the Webbing Cloak still dangling from his fingers. His fingers were knobbly, all gnarled up—Lou supposed—from decades of adventures.

Adventures that he'd only heard the very surface of.

"I believe," Auch'ray said, "that if we all stand together, if we show him just what strength we possess—and show him that we're willing to defend the Crystal City—*then* I believe that we shall all have a chance of overcoming him."

Lou had one more question, though he was afraid to ask it. He had spent his whole time as an apprentice mage trying to get over his fears—to stop being a *coward*. And he knew that what he had to ask now would make him seem just like that.

A coward.

"Why . . . why can't you fight him?" Lou said. "Wouldn't you be able to take the magical artefacts and fight him off?"

Auch'ray's eyes seemed a little glassy in the moonlight, and Lou only realised then that his master was on the brink of tears. He blinked a couple of times, drying up his eyes, as if he'd shaken off some vision that had taken place just before his nose, and then he shifted his gaze back onto Lou.

"The magical artefacts, if I was to use them, why, they would destroy me. They would tear me apart from the inside, crush my bones, crumble them up, *freeze* my blood."

His eyes lingered over Lou's once more. "You have to stop thinking that because you are young, because you are *callow*, that you do not have power, Louson, you have to believe that you *can* beat him." A new steel seemed to enter Auch'ray's eyes in that moment. "Do you really believe that I arrived into being without so much as lifting a finger? That I earned my powers without hard work. Without dedication. Without doing *frightening* things?"

That word he mentioned, the 'frightening' part, told Lou all he needed to know. That if Auch'ray hadn't read his mind, then at least he had easily been able to read Lou's expression. He knew just what he was thinking . . . or how he felt.

"Louson," Auch'ray said, "for every ice mage there comes a time to either sink or swim, and this may very well be yours."

29

TROUBLE ON THE HORIZON

A S THE EARLY MORNING LIGHT peeled back the night, the cursed animals skittered for the shadows. They scrabbled and lolloped in their ragged packs, their fur ripped and knitted with blood. Their paws padded along the slightly damp earth as they headed for the trees, for the forests, where they would hide out till the twilight came.

A light scent of dew carried on the breeze, belying the promise of blood to be had that day, and the cold bite to the wind suggested the dying remnants of the night. Those chilled mountain winds scurrying back to the Sable Mountains, and off the plains.

From the ramparts, Lou watched as the fog slunk back from the plains surrounding Ilsnare, dissipated in the air, and he wondered what the world might look like once Ma'reygar was through with it.

If he managed to defeat them.

Would he choke the whole of the kingdom with that same fog,

once he got his hands back on the magical artefacts in Lou's possession?

Or would he simply consolidate, make Ilsnare some kind of magical fortress that none dared penetrate?

And would Lou stand beside him or would he be cast out, or killed?

There was no reason for thinking that Ma'reygar would show him any mercy.

He reached into his cloak and pulled out the jar of Boonurksdale. He peeled off the lid and dipped his fingers inside, like a child would, and brought out a dab of the goo. He sucked on it, tasting that tangerine goo, and the blackberry and hazelnut thicken over his tongue.

Somehow it made him pine for the Sable Mountains.

For when things had been simpler.

When there hadn't been wars to be fought.

Though he'd only thought to consume a little of the jam, he ended up finishing it all, finally laying the emptied jar at his feet.

He gazed off around him, to the ramparts, to the Royal Guards all crouched down, keeping themselves out of the line of sight, so that any of Ma'reygar's scouts who might be looking on from the plains wouldn't be able to count them.

There were perhaps a thousand men, all told, all of them in those neat, nicely pressed grey uniforms, all of them clutching their crossbows, ready to let fly at a moment's notice. Their daggers were snuggled down at their thighs and they each had a sword and a shield slung over their shoulders.

Lou wished that he was as well armed.

Though Herimyre had wanted his, Auch'ray's and the monks' help, he hadn't been so desperate—or so naïve—as to grant Lou access to the magical artefacts.

The only two it appeared he knew of, in any case, were the Webbing Blade and the Webbing Bow.

Herimyre had no idea that Lou had the Webbing Cloak stuffed into the back of his trousers, and that he could feel its ice magic send a shimmering tingle up his spine, and the ice magic in his veins prickling all round his circulatory system.

Neither did Herimyre have any idea of how much the Webbing Cloak frightened Lou.

That he was too afraid to so much as shrug it over his shoulders.

Terrified of what it might do.

Of what it might turn him into.

Off along the ramparts, Lou spied the huddled forms of the monks. The way they all crowded together reminded him of chickens all bunching up for warmth. He caught Flucknor's eye among them, and Lou returned his nervous smile.

The young, blond monk would surely learn a lesson today.

Perhaps one to put his experience of the raid on Ravensbark in the shade.

Lou turned his attention back to the horizon, to the very furthest point that he could see and, almost simultaneously—at least Lou couldn't recall which happened first—with Lou spotting the first silhouette on the horizon, a long, flat bugle call echoed about the walls of Ilsnare Palace.

At first Lou was certain that there was only one figure slinking towards them. In the shimmering sunrise—that rounded, pinkish glow—he could hardly make out the finer details.

But, as the apparently single figure drew closer, Lou saw that he had been incorrect in his assumption.

It wasn't a single figure at all.

It was a column.

A column of mages.

All headed right for them.

Lou glanced back along the ramparts. The guards all remained ducked down beneath the stone wall. Lou caught another whiff of that fresh dew smell on the breeze. This time, though, there was nothing refreshing about it.

Nothing revitalising.

It sent a tingle of anticipation through his gut, and he found himself reaching for the inside of his cloak again, before he realised that he'd eaten his way through all his jam.

Now he had to stand up to this onslaught without aid.

Just his physical body and his magic.

He glanced off to his left, and picked out Sully and Rut.

Both of them had been fitted out with their own set of Royal Guards' uniforms, and it was still odd for Lou to see them in those pale-grey tones, as if they had defected.

And then Lou reminded himself that they had *all* defected.

Sully and Rut stood at the head of the rest of Lou's people, men and women all dressed in those same pale grey uniforms, all of them clutching their crossbows and swords assigned them.

That same morning Lou had insisted that Syre stay behind, that she remain up in his bedroom in the tower. And she'd agreed, finally. Though that apparently hadn't put his nerves to rest since he'd spent a long while looking off among his people, as if he might catch sight of her face there.

Defying his orders once again.

Lou turned his attention back to the approaching invaders.

The way they formed up. Walked straight for them. Headed right for the walls of the city. Fearless. It sent another shudder through Lou's blood.

Because he knew that the only factor which stood behind such a gesture was pure, unadulterated confidence.

They were confident that they would win the day.

And they had no qualms whatsoever of showing their hand.

Lou braced himself. Gripped tight to the stone rampart. Felt his weathered palms slot into the rough surface. And he waited. Heart in mouth. Blood pumping.

He had no weapons other than his magic.

. . . Aside from the Webbing Cloak, of course.

Just as Herimyre had briefed them that morning, not one guard moved a muscle until the invaders had reached the outskirts of the wall. Till they came into range.

And then, with a sharp, tuneless whistle, the guards all rose as one.

Crossbow bolts flurried through the air.

They tore to their targets.

And stopped dead, apparently in mid-air.

Lou gawped as he looked down on the invaders, surely about the same numbers as theirs. A thousand or so. All spread out. An impossibly long line, almost. And he watched the iridescent sheen bubble out around them. And those crossbow bolts skitter to the ground.

Harmless.

Commotion broke out on the wall.

Lou's heart sunk into his chest. It beat harder. He gripped the stone wall tighter. He waited for the command. For the command from Herimyre, standing over Lou's shoulder, a few storeys up so as to have a good view of the battlefield.

But it didn't come.

And so Lou gave it himself.

"Duck!" he shouted out.

Just in time, the guards responded.

So wrapped up in his own order, Lou almost forgot to follow it himself. But that crimson bolt, webbed with luminous blue served as an effective reminded.

He dropped down. Caught his chin on the stone. Felt blood welling up to his face. And his heart skitter in his chest.

He listened to the almighty *crack* above their heads. Like the sound of a hundred trees struck by a single, enormous lightning bolt.

The air filled with the stench of ash.

And the icy chill wormed up Lou's nostrils.

Lou waited out the time. Counted his heartbeats as they struck.

One.

Two.

Three.

Four.

Five.

And then he glanced back. To the tower. To where the hex had hit.

And he saw the smoking hole in the stone wall.

For a moment he grew desperate, looked about for Herimyre.

That was where it had struck. Just where Herimyre had been standing.

Was he gone?

Lou felt a mixture of emotions descend on him.

Shock.

Confusion.

Anger.

Disappointment.

Relief.

Yes, that was right. He was *relieved*. After all, Herimyre had been the one to order his death. Surely he should feel glad that he was gone.

That he was *dead*.

But then, through the smoking hole, Lou observed a figure rise. It passed as if in a dream. No, just like the nightmare he had suffered for weeks after killing the king.

Herimyre stood silhouetted by the lapping flames. And he held his sword tight in his fist. Thrust it up in the air.

Tysron.

Time seemed to slow once more. And he knew what it meant. Knew that it was his magic. That he was being given an opportunity. Another chance.

Without thinking, he reached back, to the back of his trousers, and he felt for the rough, frayed material of the Webbing Cloak there.

And he slipped it out from under his waistline.

Brought it tight in his grip.

He clasped his eyes shut as he brought the cloak over his head. Felt the material brush against his skin.

And bathed himself in the heart-wrenching chill.

30

COMING OF AGE

LOU FELT THE WEBBING CLOAK cling to his frame. And he felt the ice magic dance across his skin. He was afraid that the magic within him—in his blood—might seep out from his skin.

And then he was afraid it might simply burst right out.

Cut *through* bone and skin to dampen the cloak.

Lou ground his teeth. Turned his concentration to control.

Control.

Control.

Control.

The magic hummed about him. Like a ball. He felt it all settle at his solar plexus. His heart hammered so hard that he was certain it would give way.

Fail completely.

Or that it would bust right out of his ribs.

He gripped the material of the Webbing Cloak all the tighter.

Glared down on the invaders nestled within that protective charm of theirs. An *enormous* protective charm.

And then he felt a slight smirk dance over his lips.

Madness?

Tingling of crazy urges?

Loss of . . . of control?

No!

Lou wrenched his grip tighter. He *would* control. He was determined. He would hold on. And he would succeed. He would be the victor here.

He would fight off *Ma'reygar!*

A crooked tremble took hold of his whole body. Seemed to shake him right down to his bones. Seemed to frazzle his blood. Seemed to warp his heart.

He felt his body becoming insignificant.

Delicate.

Lighter than the breeze.

Floating.

Was he floating?

Really?

Only when he looked down.

Down to the stone wall beneath his feet.

To the guards firing their desperate crossbow bolts.

Did he see . . . ?

Yes, he was floating.

Flying!

. . . Above them all.

Lou felt himself bursting upwards.

Higher and higher.

Into the clouds.

The dirty-bottomed clouds setting in on this otherwise flaw-less day.

This *bloodied* day.

And he felt his eardrums go *pop!* and his heart threaten to do the same.

The cloak enveloped him. All of him. Like the skin he had left behind.

His mind seemed soon to follow.

Spiralling upwards.

Faster and faster.

That smell of dewy grass still thick in his nostrils.

That burning ash. And the chill of ice.

Slowing now.

Growing slower.

Closer to the sun.

The blinding, bright, swirling sun.

None of the prickling on his skin.

Or the maddening throb in his brain.

No migraine threatening to dawn.

The cloak protected him from all.

He felt himself coming to a halt. As his head thrust through yet another cloud, he found himself face to face with two familiar people.

His ma and pa.

Beyond.

Had he gone beyond?

Slipped off the face of the Earth, gone . . . *elsewhere?*

He looked to his parents. His pa's spindly frame. His balding head. His flaking scalp.

And then his ma.

Her rosy-red cheeks. That layer of perspiration on her brow. And her barrel shape.

They smiled at him.

Thick, hearty grins.

Mouths whipped into rigid curves.

And Lou found himself smiling back.

His brain seemed to blink within his skull. Like its memories were popping, one by one.

Like he was *dying.*

But he could stay here forever. Could smile at them forever. Things were simpler up here, up here in the clouds . . . *forever.*

The whiteness got brighter. And the sun all the hotter.

Lou felt that same skitter of magic through him.

Passing through his veins.

Wrangling his heart.

Pushing it down.

Down to his gut.

And he was falling.

Again.

Back down.

Down to Earth.

~

Lou had enough awareness about him to bend his knees when he landed.

And he caught himself.

Everything was black, though.

It was night out.

Then he remembered he had his eyes shut.

And he opened them.

The ramparts were thick with the rush of activity. Guards bobbing back and forth. Their mouths whipped up into a panic. Crossbow bolts flew through the air.

Men and women shrieked.

Down below, Lou saw now, that the invaders, that Ma'reygar's army, were making their way forwards, making ground on the wall of the city.

Soon they would be through it.

And inside.

Remembering himself, Lou glanced back, back over his shoulder.

He looked for Herimyre.

But didn't see him there.

Disappeared.

Feeling the Webbing Cloak tight about him, Lou sprinted off along the rampart, dodging the guards as they tried to get by him.

To fire yet more of their worthless bolts at the intruders.

Lou had to be fast if he was to save them all.

31

A FRAUGHT MELEE

L OU RUSHED DOWN the spiral steps that led off the ramparts.

Quiet here.

Much quieter.

Here he could hear the tread of his boots. He leaped down the steps. Heard the *slap-slap-slap* of his steps.

The *thud-thud* of his heart drained his thoughts.

The *piff-piff* of the crossbow bolts overhead thrust him on.

And soon he was back on ground level.

On the same level as the intruders.

As Ma'reygar himself.

He trod quickly, hugging the stone walls of the palace. Nipped his way through the primly cut lawns, now singed with cast-off hexes.

With fire and ice magic.

He made it out onto the cobblestones of the main street. The street which led to the gate. He felt the Webbing Cloak surround him. Its subtle influence act on him.

Making him spry, almost as quick as to be invisible.

But, more than anything else, he felt the weight of the magic on his shoulders. Like a boulder that threatened to crush him beneath its load.

And yet he resisted.

Found the strength to resist.

He glanced to the gate. Still standing up. Shut.

And he knew that he couldn't go there.

Not yet.

First he needed the magical artefacts.

The Webbing Blade.

And the Webbing Bow.

Then he would be a force to be reckoned with.

The Webbing Cloak would see to that.

As his mind chided him forwards, his mottled muscles and bones cried out for him to stop. For him to rest his hurting body.

Lou felt the pain pulsing from where he'd struck his chin.

But he cast it aside.

He cast all else aside.

If the magic was to kill him today, then so be it.

At least it would be in the service of saving his people.

And the people of Ilsnare.

Because, without a doubt in his mind, he knew that magic —*unchecked* magic—was the scourge of the kingdom.

And it was up to him to prevent it.

As Lou pounded his way through the city, past all the shuttered-up windows and doors, the citizens of Ilsnare hiding out to await the result of the siege, Lou realised that he had no idea just where he was headed.

Where he might be going at all.

With that thought on his mind, he caught sight of the hefty figure of Herimyre, leaping out from within one of the towers.

The tower which had been struck by the hex.

And he grasped his sword.

Tysron.

Herimyre landed before Lou. He stood with his nostrils flaring. His face red. Damp with sweat. A cut bleeding freely from just above his eyebrow. Blood pooling down over his left eye.

But he was alive.

He had survived the hex.

And he still had his sword.

Herimyre glowered out at Lou. His lips curled back into a snarl. "*You!*" he said. "Death too good for you, eh? To die alongside the honest falling bodies of my men? Couldn't hack it up on the ramparts?"

Lou felt his heart throb in his throat. Because he had reasons. *Real* reasons. But he saw that, right now, Herimyre would certainly not be receptive to them.

That he was blinded by pain and rage.

And a thirst for blood.

Before Lou could get out a single syllable, Herimyre swung Tysron hard and fast through the air.

Lou thought himself dead.

Nothing to be done.

But, somehow, the Webbing Cloak carried him.

As a breeze carries a leaf.

And he dodged the strike.

This only served to infuriate Herimyre all the more. And he swung again.

This time, though, with the aid of the Webbing Cloak, Lou was faster on his feet still, and he dodged around the raging king. And he skittered off deeper into the city, losing himself with great speed among the sprawling, labyrinthine backstreets.

Only then did Lou give in to the urge to rest.

He held his hand out and rested against a stone wall of a house.

Another shuttered-up house.

And, unable to help it, he thought of Hildie again.

How she'd had a house just like this one.

Lou cast off the thought just as quickly as he realised he was having it. And he glanced back over his shoulder.

Footsteps?

Could he still hear footsteps?

He was almost certain.

Perhaps Herimyre, seeing that the battle was futile, that it couldn't be won, had decided to pursue Lou.

To take him with him.

And to at least strike him down.

Lou felt his chest tighten. He stared at the corner of the street, ready to see Herimyre's great bulk turn the corner. For him to brandish Tysron, clenched in his fist and ready to strike him.

And yet he didn't come.

But the footsteps continued to sound.

Finally, someone did turn the corner.

Not Herimyre, though.

No. Not him at all.

Syre.

∾

Lou met those eyes of hers, and took in her inky black hair. Her face was creased with the effort of her running. And now, he saw, also from the effort of what she carried.

She held a bundle in her arms.

As she drew closer, Lou had no need to ask her just what she held there. What she had brought to him.

But, even as he unravelled the bundle, he couldn't quite bring himself to believe—to *truly* believe—what he saw nestled inside.

The Webbing Blade.

The Webbing Bow.

And a good helping of arrows.

She had snaffled them back. Got them back for him. Rescued them from wherever Herimyre had confiscated them to.

Lou wrenched them from her grasp almost too quickly for her to realise it. He slung the Bow over his shoulder and gripped the Blade tight, down at his side.

So here he was now.

The fully fitted-out Spider Warrior.

Would the magic corrupt him too?

Just as it had Xeda?

Or would he be able to resist?

He felt the urge pulling at his solar plexus, dragging him onwards. But he resisted. It was calling to him. Calling him to battle. To put an end to this magical *squabble* . . . because that was all it was, wasn't it?

He was the Spider Warrior.

The sun no longer pounded him. In fact, it seemed to retreat from him, behind a cloud, like a terrified lamb, trying to take cover in its mother's wool.

No . . . *breathe* . . . *breathe* . . . *breathe* . . .

Lou caught himself.

Caught his thoughts.

Stopped himself getting carried away.

Beneath all this. Stripped of the magical artefacts. Of his magical blood.

He was just a mortal, like anyone else.

He had to remember that.

Or it would destroy him.

He refound his mortal mind. Allowed himself back into it. And he fixed Syre in his stare. "How?" he said. "How did you get them?"

But she had no need to answer. That pit-black flash which swept her eyes was enough for him to know the truth. To know just how she had taken care of whoever had guarded the artefacts.

But, now, with the Webbing Blade, Bow and Cloak in his possession, Lou would *save* many more lives.

He was *sure* of it.

Without another word to Syre, he padded off, along the cobblestones, and back out into the thick of battle.

32

A HERO'S STAND

LOU COULD FEEL his pulse racing all the quicker as he padded through the streets of the city. As he eyed the gates up ahead of him. Unmanned now, of course. And, he realised a second later, shattered by an enormous, smoking hole.

The shrieks and cries returned to him.

But made no impact.

He supposed, had he been feeling in a more *mortal* mood, they might've had some effect on him. But, as it was, he felt calm. At peace. Resting, almost.

So complete was his trust in his power that he knew that he would be able to pummel any force at all into submission.

Parry it back to where it had come from.

He did not run. He marched, sure and proud, out to the gaping hole in the wooden gates. And, as if stepping through a thicket to gather berries—as he had done as a boy, when he had been a working hand—he headed through the gate and out onto the plains.

The air was filled with colours. And sparks. And smoke. And ice.

Mages and guards battled on. Some on the ramparts. Others down on the plains. Fighting hard against the pit-black wall. Almost lost in its obsidian tone.

And then the plains before him.

Littered with bodies.

Mages.

Cloaks furled about them like wood curled up in flames.

Guards.

Dressed in their pale grey uniforms.

Mouths latched open.

Eyes wide.

Wounds bleeding freely.

Dead.

Lou saw them all. Smelled that blood. Tasted it, even. But, over everything else, he caught the whiff of the ethereal scent of the Webbing Cloak.

Of that dank, bloody odour.

But he felt it comfort him now.

Settle his heart.

Still his pulse.

And with calmness on his mind, he shifted his gaze off, to take in the plains, to take in the battle.

And he saw them.

All three of them.

Locked in battle.

Herimyre.

Auch'ray.

Ma'reygar.

Lou bided his time. Like a cursed wolf circling a campfire. Picking its moment. Waiting for the right time to step in and ravage its unsuspecting victims.

Because they had to die.

All three of them.

That was the way it would be.

To save his people.

That was the cost.

Lou watched their hexes spiral through the air. And he watched Herimyre, on the defensive, clutching Tysron tight in his fist, parrying the magic, firing it back at Ma'reygar, and Auch'ray conjuring spells of his own to hurl at him.

All of them locked in a fight to the death.

But now it was Lou's turn.

His turn to show them the true superior of them all.

To show them that the Spider Warrior had returned.

. . . If he had ever really been gone.

Lou drank it all in. The magic surrounding him. He channelled it with the Webbing Cloak. *Sucked* it all up. It glowed within him. And flowed through him. Into his blood. Out through his heart. Up to his brain. And then down, down.

Down again.

To the pit of his stomach.

And then to his solar plexus.

For the longest time, he allowed it to linger there.

He *held* it there.

Controlling the brute magical force.

Refusing to allow it to overwhelm him.

And then, with a toying simplicity, he let it go.

That was when the voice struck him.

The familiar voice.

Hildie.

But it was too late.

Too late for her.

Because he had done what was required of him.

What his people required of him.

33

A MAGICAL OUTPOURING

LOU CLASPED HIS EYES SHUT as he felt the magic ebb out from him. Surround him. Linger about him like a thickening fog. And he felt it dance over the ground, like skittering sparks off the head of an axe which strikes a rock.

It danced over his veins.

And through his heart.

Tickled his lungs.

Drew his nerves tight.

And singed his muscles.

Only when he tasted the blood in his mouth did he realise it was his own. That he had been biting on his tongue, that his teeth had sunk right into its soft surface.

His cheeks, too, burned with pain.

But, all that, and whatever other pains he might've had, were dulled into nothingness with the numbness of ice which ripped through him.

Soothing and numbing in equal measure.

But it wasn't the ice that brought him round.

That prompted him to open his eyes and take in his surroundings.

No, it was the crushing silence.

All round him.

Pounding him from all sides, like an oppressive, low-lying thunderstorm, about to break at any moment.

And so he opened his eyes.

Just like the others. Their bodies lay on their backs. Mouths latched open. Eyes blank and staring.

All three of them.

Herimyre.

Auch'ray.

Ma'reygar.

All of them dead now.

The ones that he had killed. That he had wielded his power against.

And, for the longest time, Lou just stared at them, awed by his power. Awed at how it had flowed through him.

And then out of him.

Taken all three of these men down.

He turned his attention to Herimyre's sword. To Tysron. Its blade melted steel. Now locked to its bearer's chest. And Lou knew that it hadn't been able to resist the mighty power he wielded. That he had managed to reforge it.

Slowly the world ticked back into life around Lou.

He blinked away his daze as if coming round from a nightmare.

He could feel the jostle of activity about him. Mutterings among the groans of pain.

When he turned on his heel, looked back off over his shoulder, he saw the guards, all that remained living and breathing, shuffling about on the ramparts. Others trudged about down on the plains.

All of them stayed at a safe distance from Lou.

And he was glad. Because he could still feel the tingle of the lingering magic within him. Still threatening to burst right out from him.

He had to keep it inside.

Further away, he watched the mages disappearing, fleeing now that they'd lost their commander. Headed back for the Sable Mountains with their tails between their legs.

And Lou was glad.

If Ilsnare needed one thing, it was a break from magic.

Just for a while.

There was no way of knowing how long he stood there. Rooted to the spot. Staring at his dead master, and his two adversaries. The two men who had been on his thoughts for the longest time.

It had been easy in the end.

He had simply had to channel the raw magic, and it had taken its course.

It had chewed them up and left them there, prostrate.

The dank stench of blood from the Webbing Cloak still hung about him and, somewhere off in the back of his mouth, there was still the suggestion of that jam. Of the Boonurksdale he had taken before the invaders had arrived at the city walls.

That seemed long ago now.

Not just a matter of an hour or so.

And he knew that he could never get back that time again.

But the tingle, the sharp taste of the blackberries and the hazelnuts remained. Went some way to soothing him. To reminding him that he was still alive.

A living and breathing person.

Was he even mortal any longer?

Lou felt her fingertips on his forearm. He flinched at her touch. At the heat that emanated out from her skin and onto his. And, slowly, he turned to face her. Met her eyes with his.

Emerald eyes. Flame-red hair. Delicate, porcelain skin.

Hildie.

They regarded one another for a long moment, her fingers still touching his forearm, like the gentle stirring of coals in a simmering fireplace. But he could resist her. He knew that he had the power to resist her.

But could the same be said for her being able to resist him?

"I'm sorry," Lou said, his words sounding flat and awkward as they passed his lips.

Hildie broke off his gaze and then looked out over to where the dead bodies lay.

To Herimyre, Auch'ray and Ma'reygar.

Though Lou could see her forehead was creased and her gaze distant, he saw no anger there. Neither any outright display of sadness. No grief.

At least not yet.

"It's okay," she answered finally, "I guess, in some way, it had to be like this."

"I couldn't let your father go through with his plans, he . . . he wanted to hurt my people. And I just couldn't allow it."

She nodded glumly then glanced back at him, her eyes meeting his for a fleeting second. "I'm glad it's over."

"What now?" Lou said.

"What d'you mean?"

Lou cast a glance back over his shoulder, back to the walls of Ilsnare, to those pit-black walls which loomed high over them. "Who's going to take charge around here with neither Herimyre or Ma'reygar the victor in the battle?"

Hildie parted her lips to speak and then her eyes shifted off his, and she looked off over his shoulder, behind him.

He followed her gaze, up to where she was looking.

To the ramparts.

To the guards there.

They'd all stopped gathering up their dead, or firing off the last of the useless bolts after the fleeing mages. Now they were all staring down at him, at him and Hildie.

When Hildie spoke, her lips were unsmiling, her tone flat and grave. "It looks like the next leader of Ilsnare is much closer than we think."

Lou broke off his observation of those guards, all up there on the ramparts, and he looked back over the dead bodies. "I want them all given a decent burial"—he locked eyes with Hildie once again—"a *hero's* burial, all three of them."

When he looked back at Hildie again, he observed the springing of tears about the corners of her eyes. "Whatever you say, Your Highness."

34

A KING IS CROWNED

L OU SAT ABOUT in the king's chambers. The chambers that had once, a long time ago now it seemed, belonged to the man he had killed ... and then to Herimyre.

He liked to keep the doors to the veranda wide open so that the wind off the Sable Mountains drifted into his chamber, floated about. Whenever people had asked about it, asked if he wanted the doors shut to guard against a chill, he had got touchy about it. They had soon learned not to ask such questions.

The real reason he liked to feel the breeze of the Sable Mountains had less to do with dewy-eyed remembrance: for his travels, for Auch'ray, for Ravensbark, and more to do with taking out the dank stench of blood which seemed to cling to him.

And that stench still followed him despite the fact he had had all the magical artefacts sealed away deep in the vaults of Ilsnare Palace.

Locked the Webbing Cloak, and its distinctive smell, far away.

The trimmings of his quarters were wonderful too, he

supposed. There was the four-poster bed, with its light grey hang-ings—the ones that reminded him of the uniform of the Royal Guards—and he had a whole lounge-set off to one side of his quarters, complete with an elegant, tasselled rope that he only had to tug to summon a servant to see to his every want and need.

Yes, it was a good life.

A *pampered* life.

If that was the one he wanted.

Because, when he looked out of those veranda windows, he could hardly see past those patterned emerald drapes to the Sable Mountains on the horizon.

Those emerald drapes reminded him of Hildie's eyes.

And, the more he thought about it, it seemed an awfully long time since he had seen Hildie.

The past few weeks had been long and tedious, it had seemed. Nothing at all that he could've convinced himself to believe at the beginning of his journey—back when he had been Lou the Working Hand.

Or even when he had become Louson Dorf the Ice Mage.

No, now everything had been shifted about, thrown all over the place.

It had been like one of those tides, one of those that lapped at the banks of Shildersmoore that he had noted while waiting for the boat out to Brinder Island.

He had been carried along with everything else. Nodded when asked questions. Glared at people when it had seemed they needed frightening.

Because, and this was one thing that stuck with him, *everyone* was afraid of him.

They had either witnessed first-hand his powers out on the plains or they had heard the stories.

And being feared did not sit well with him.

This would've been just how Ma'reygar would have ruled.

No, more and more, Lou had been spending time up in his quarters, away from the pomp and gilt of day-to-day royal life.

And that suited him just fine.

Things had changed dramatically in terms of the administration and governance of Ilsnare.

At first, when the wise men, or whatever their official titles had been, had come to him, he had told them that he didn't want to be king.

But they had insisted.

Told him there was no other option.

That if he gave up the throne then Ilsnare would descend into anarchy.

In the end they had struck a deal, completely changed the charter of the kingdom. They had decided that, rather than before, where the king had written laws and put them into practice, now there would be a council—much like the *Magical* Council, in many ways—which would see its way to deciding on all matters of state.

It would all be democratic.

Controlled by the citizens of Ilsnare's votes.

And Lou would only be a figurehead.

A *head* of state.

Someone for the people to look up to, to use as a symbol.

And, Lou was most adamant about this part, someone to protect them.

Because his power was awesome. He could admit that without subjectivity now. And, in any case, no one would dispute *that* claim.

He had destroyed, in one fell swoop, not one, but *three* of the most powerful men of the age. And not even the Spider Warrior had been able to dispose of Ma'reygar.

In a way, Lou felt like he had done Xeda's biding.

Finished the job he would've relished doing.

But, the main thing for Lou was that the kingdom was struck in some kind of peace. There was, once again, equilibrium to life.

One of his only contributions to that wise men's council had been the ordering of the villages of the plains to be rebuilt, to have them all put back together so that the people could go back to their ordinary lives.

His hometown, Endmere ,would be rebuilt, among others.

Killing Ma'reygar had disposed of the curse which had hung onto Ilsnare for so many years.

There was no need for skullers any longer.

And so Lou had appointed Sully and Rut to serve as his most senior generals in the Royal Guards. And any other man or woman from his people would be appointed to the Royal Guards who asked it.

Because, now Lou had to admit it, to understand it, everyone in the entire stretch of the Crystal City—*no*, in the whole of the Kingdom of Shellacnass: the Crystal Kingdom—was now *his* people.

And he had no intention of letting any of them down.

Of leaving them for one second unprotected.

That was his duty now.

Just as Lou turned to look over the patterned emerald drapes for what was perhaps the dozenth time that day, he heard a rapping at the sturdy, oak door to his quarters.

He summoned the knocker in.

Guilknot. His personal errand boy. Pale-faced and bony.

"Yes?" Lou said.

"The monks," Guilknot said. "They're leaving, Your Highness."

Lou took a final glance of the patterned emerald drapes and then broke away from them. He managed to raise a smile to Guilknot. "I'd best see them off then, hadn't I?"

Lou followed Guilknot's hurried heels down the steps, listening to the soles of his shoes *pitter-patter* against the stone, and he found something sticking in his throat.

Was it sadness? Sadness at seeing the monks leaving?

Or was it relief that things were going back to normal, just when he had believed nothing would be normal again?

He had little time to pin it down, because before he knew it he was turning to corner and emerging out into the courtyard.

The midday sun beamed down on the collected horses, and their loads all harnessed up on their backs, tied up with thick ropes. Some of them whinnied while others dozed lazily. The smell of horse sweat and manure rose off them.

Lou felt a slight tingle at the back of his throat which reminded him why he hadn't ever *really* liked horses.

He picked out Damon Shriversmyth almost right away, standing at the head of the procession, the procession that was about to leave, and he headed up to him. "Everything packed up and ready, then?" Lou said.

Damon raised a smile to him. "I think so, Your Highness."

Lou batted his hand. "Don't worry about that title stuff, we're friends after all. And you know as well as I do that it means absolutely nothing. I'm not the one in power here. Not *really*."

"All the same," Damon said, reaching out to shake his hand, "I can fairly say that my opinion of you has changed somewhat over these seasons."

"For better or worse?"

Damon shrugged. "A bit of both, I suppose."

They both chuckled.

"You take care," Lou said. "And don't forget that you're all welcome here if the building doesn't go as planned, if you find the winter nipping at your heels. You can always pass the winter here."

Damon grinned. "Very kind of you, Your Highness, and an offer that I won't likely forget in a hurry. Though I think it would be best for us—*all* of us—to start up afresh. Bringing balance back to the magical equilibrium. And, unfortunately, that'll mean us seeing much less of one another."

"Yeah," Lou said, his eyes skittering off along the procession, and then picking out Hildie. His heart jumped up to his throat as he turned his attention back to Damon. "I suppose that's just the new normal, I mean, monks sticking with monks, and mages . . . well, ruling over mortals."

Damon smirked, reached out and clapped Lou on the shoulder. "As long as you keep up this benevolent streak of yours I reckon you'll be just fine. Don't go getting too big for your boots, that's all I'm saying."

Lou smiled back, wished Damon a safe journey and then proceeded down the procession to where he had seen Hildie, up on the saddle of one of the horses, and as ready as any of the monks to head on out.

She kept facing forwards, the hood of her cloak covering her head and steeping her face in shadow. But Lou could still catch the odd glimmer of that flame-red hair of hers.

Over the past few weeks Lou had seen nothing of Hildie. The

last time he had seen her, in fact, had been at her father— Ma'rey-gar's—funeral. And even then they hadn't spoken.

He guessed that she was avoiding him.

And he couldn't blame her.

Surely she was angry with him, and that would take time to shift.

If it ever shifted at all.

"You're leaving too?" Lou said.

Hildie remained facing forwards, her eyes fixed just beyond the tip of her nose. She nodded, her cloak creasing a little as she did so.

Lou glanced off along the procession, picked out Flucknor a few monks back, standing alongside his horse, ready to lead it along the hard road back to the Sable Mountains, and then to rebuild Ravensbark.

But at least he wouldn't have to contend with cursed animals.

"Look," Lou said, "I'm truly sorry about how things happened —but you must see that there was no other way. And"—he paused a moment trying to think of the right way to express himself —"you managed to stop the magical war. Thousands and thousands of lives were spared."

Hildie said nothing, however, she just kept on facing forwards in the saddle. He watched as slowly her hands appeared out from the sleeves of her cloak, and those dainty fingers of hers clasped hold of the front of the saddle, as if the horse might be about to break into a gallop.

Just as Lou was on the point of moving on, to leaving Hildie in peace, she tilted her head around, met his eyes with hers—with those *emerald* eyes—and Lou couldn't find any way to break off their eye contact.

It was as if she held him in a spell.

Far more powerful than any her father might've cast.

He watched, numbed, as her fingers slipped from the saddle and grabbed him, as they stuck into his hair and held on tight. She dragged his mouth up to meet hers. And, in that moment, he was lost to the softness of her lips. And the sweetness of her breath.

And a slight—very slight—taste of ash.

Then, just like that, it was over. She withdrew from him, and Lou saw that Damon had kicked the procession into action, that they were moving out. Directed towards the Sable Mountains. But, before Hildie's horse followed along with the others, she dug into her cloak and withdrew a letter—sallow, weather-stained parchment, with several blots of ink covering it.

Lou just about snatched it from her grasp as her horse followed on with the procession.

"What's this?" Lou said, trotting alongside, managing to keep up with the procession as it snaked out of the courtyard, and headed out onto the plains.

Hildie shrugged, met his eye a moment, then said, "My father had it hidden in his cloak."

And, just like that, she disappeared off around the corner, and out onto the plains.

Gone from sight.

Leaving Lou just clutching the letter in his fist.

With Hildie leaving, the rest of the world had near enough dimmed into incomprehension for Lou, and it was only when he heard Flucknor calling out to him that he remembered that he was even there.

And the matter was made even more confusing still when Flucknor brought his horse to a halt, and slipped off his saddle, his boots landing with a pair of *thuds*. His eyes were wide and his mouth wide open. And Lou could only make out the words he spoke after he had said a few sentences.

"... Please let me stay here," Flucknor said, "I promise that I can contribute something. I ... I ..."

Lou held up his hand, thoroughly confused. "What're you saying? Start from the beginning, won't you?"

Flucknor took several breaths, glanced off at the procession, now disappearing off around the corner, and onto the plains.

Gone forever, as far as Lou was concerned.

"Will you take me on?" Flucknor said.

"What?"

"As your apprentice?"

Lou had to admit he was rendered more stunned by the question than the context, though, of course, Flucknor being a monk—having committed himself to being a monk—the whole proposal was ridiculous from the start.

"Why, uh, I ..."

"Don't say you're not ready," Flucknor said. "Because you and I both know that's not true at all. You're the most powerful mage in the world. You killed two of the strongest mages ever to live."

If Lou had thought to argue, he might've claimed that it was in no small part due to the magical artefacts he'd had at his disposal. But the fact remained that he was just dumbstruck by the nature of the request.

"Uh," he said, and then snapped back to something resembling logical thought, "okay, well, as long as Damon says that it's okay."

Flucknor's eyes lit up and he seemed caught in two minds. Not sure where to run. And then his body seemed to catch up with his mind, because he skittered off.

Lou watched Flucknor disappear around the corner, just like the rest of the monks—and Hildie—had done, and then he made inroads on opening the letter. When he unfolded the parchment, he read:

Brother Lou,

I'm asking Ma'reygar to deliver this letter to you so that you can know the truth of the matter, so that you can know that I'm quite all right. That Ma'reygar doesn't blame me for leading you to the Threaded Pit. Nor for having hidden your escape.

But he is coming for you, Lou, though I believe that much shall become clear soon enough, since when you receive this letter it shall be at Ma'reygar's hand.

So, I suppose all that's left is to tell you to take care, brother, and that you keep out of danger's way as far as you can.

I suppose, in many ways, it'll be a blessing if you never get to read this letter.

Take care, brother,

Lunthard

Lou felt his chest tighten and his heart begin to hammer. He had been so sure that Ma'reygar would have killed Lunthard. He had had no reason to keep him alive, especially after he had deceived him so horribly.

Allowed the magical artefacts to slip through his fingers.

Perhaps Ma'reygar was less of a monster than Lou had imagined.

Maybe Lou hadn't been seeing the whole picture.

Then again, Lou thought, recalling Hildie's story of her parents, he supposed that the main motive behind Ma'reygar's hatred for the mortal realm had been because of how the king had killed his wife.

Taken his love from him.

At least now both Ma'reygar and his wife were at peace.

Though Hildie would always be far from Lou.

But perhaps it was for the best.

"What's that?"

Lou turned to see that Syre had appeared at his elbow, and he met those eyes of hers, just like he always did now, instinctively looking for that murkiness lurking there. That dark magic struggling to get out.

But today there was nothing.

He showed her the letter, watched her read it over twice, and then observed the tears rolling down her cheeks. He took it back from her as she brought her hand up to her face to dry her tears with the sleeve of her tunic.

As Lou crumpled up the letter and turned to head back up the spiral stone steps to his quarters, he heard the *slap* of sandals careening over the ground. And he turned to see Flucknor blazing around the corner.

He grinned, from ear to ear. And Lou had no need to ask him what Damon had said.

He smiled back at him, then reached forwards and ruffled his hair, and the three of them—Syre tagging along too—climbed the stone steps, up to the king's quarters.

The view from the king's chambers was one that he wanted to share forever.

Or for as long as he was king.

As long as his people needed him.

35

STARTING OVER

THE LONG GRASS SWISHED UP at the waistband of Hildie's trousers. The dew had already settled in over many of the blades and she could feel its dampness soaking into the material of her trousers, making her skin tremble.

Just a touch.

The trees were like firm friends, with their round, soft shapes, and their fertile greens.

Out here it was easy to forget.

As for forgiveness ... well, she would see.

Overhead, the sun was coming down in the sky, and she thought to herself about how tonight there would be no threat. No cursed animals to be wary of. Nothing for her to be afraid of.

And, more than anything else, she would be far from Louson Dorf, and the Crystal City.

Because, if she was true to herself, that was what scared her most.

And yet the urge to turn around, to go back there, to leap into Lou's arms, that was almost overwhelming

But equally impossible.

No, she had made her choice, the choice to stride out on her own.

She recalled the expression on Damon Shriversmyth's face as they had bid one another goodbye. Whereas before, back before *all* of this, she had considered him her unconditional friend, she had seen that something had changed between them.

That there was something nagging at Damon beneath the surface.

And she was certain that it was because he knew what she had done.

What she had *had* to do.

Burn down those villages to summon her army.

And so save her father too.

If it was to affect their relationship from that point onwards, then she supposed that there was really nothing to be done. She just had to accept it and move on with her life.

As the monks would move on with theirs.

Though she chided herself not to, she found the urge over-whelming, and she *had* to turn herself right around once again, *had* to look down onto the plains, and then to Ilsnare—to the Crystal City—as it lingered there on the horizon.

Its brutish, obsidian walls that surrounded it.

And its glass rooftops glinting in the setting sunlight.

Tonight the people of Ilsnare would sleep tight because they knew that Louson Dorf was watching over them.

The most powerful mage in the land.

Of their times.

She could hardly summon the grain of thought to imagine just what inner strength it must've taken for him to do what needed to be done . . . and then to stop.

To simply lay down his arms, and walk away.

Would she have had that required strength?

She had no way to say, though, whenever she was honest with herself, she compared herself more with the Spider Warrior—with *Xeda*—than with Lou.

Because she was *bad*, and she knew it.

Whenever Lou had killed it had been of necessity, in the service of some greater good.

When *she* had killed it had been to serve her own ego. To make herself feel better about things. To serve her own plans. To try and save her father. The last of her family.

No, the people of Ilsnare were much better off with her far away.

Where she couldn't hurt them.

These days she had found herself wondering if how things had turned out might've been how her father would've wanted.

How he had *really* wanted.

When he hadn't been struck by some fit of rage.

All he had wanted, really, was revenge. And hadn't he got that?

He had seen the king, and then Herimyre, killed.

And then he had been killed himself.

Relieved of his misery. No longer condemned to walk the world lonely and without direction. And, to Hildie, in that moment, that sounded like a mighty fine thing.

But she didn't dwell on it long.

No, the way she had to see things, how she had to see things *now*, was as an opportunity, a fresh start. She could reinvent herself far away, do whatever it was that she wanted to do. And now she could be truly free.

She had no ties.

No home.

No friends or family any longer.

And yet, right at that moment, she wished for none of those things.

Because now the world was ripe with opportunities, and things to be done.

She turned her back on the Crystal City and waded on further through the tall grass. She could feel a faint breeze blowing through the trees. She felt it cool her, just a touch.

Soon the moon would be out and she would need to find shelter.

Though Lou had learned well to walk with his weakness—and so quickly too—she was a long way off.

That was the thing with mages, the way that knowledge didn't come in the same way. Each of them had patches of unknowing. Things that came easily, and things that came hard.

Brute strength, for Lou, had come easily.

Frighteningly easily. Albeit with the aid of the magical artefacts.

Hildie, though, had patience. She would work on her magic. Get better. And then, perhaps, she could stand to be around Lou for longer, be able to tolerate his ice magic.

Reach the point where it wouldn't hurt her.

Or not.

As she strode up and over the cusp of the hill, and along the foothills of the Sable Mountains, she didn't bother to look back for a final time at Ilsnare.

Already she was certain that she could hear the sound of gulls, and smell the salty ocean on the air. Fresh fish. Now, *that* would be a fine way for her to regain her strength.

Fresh fish and the ocean breeze.

Why, it sounded just about perfect.

And so, with that thought etched on her mind, she leaped forwards, and down through the thickening grassy grove, and into the base of the valley.

Almost able to *imagine* the lap of the cool waves against her skin.

AUTHOR'S NOTE

Thank you for taking the time to read one of my books. If you would like to hear about my latest releases you can sign up for my newsletter here: www.raymondsflex.com

Thanks for reading!

Raymond S Flex

The Webbing Cloak
The Third Crystal Kingdom Novel

www.ingramcontent.com/pod-product-compliance
Lightning Source LLC
Chambersburg PA
CBHW031214260626

47169CB00007B/2053